The Vice Principals' Submissive Student

by

Anonymous

LOCUS ELM™

find more by typing

Locus_Elm_Press

at:

Amazon United Kingdom
Amazon United States of America
Amazon Germany
Amazon Netherlands
Amazon France
Amazon Spain
Amazon Canada
Amazon Australia
Amazon Brazil
Amazon Japan
Amazon Mexico
Amazon Italy
Amazon India

*

THE VICE PRINCIPALS' SUBMISSIVE STUDENT

Jennifer's Extra-Credit Erotic Education

by

Anonymous

Published: July 2017

TABLE OF CONTENTS

*

CHAPTER 1

Jennifer moaned and spread her legs wider. The finger rubbed up and down the smooth slit of her cant. Slowly, the finger neared her throbbing clit. She groaned aloud as it swiftly reversed direction before it reached her sensitive fuck nub. The finger worked down to her open cunthole, where it began softly circling the reddened rim. Her juices were flowing heavily, and the finger easily slid over the girl's slick pussy flesh.

Leaning back in the car seat and thrusting out her cunt, Jennifer panted, "Ohhhh, please, baby, rub my did" She closed her eyes as a long, low groan left her parted lips, Her clit throbbed, begging for attention. It stood out from her cunt, engorged with hot blood. Her fucknub needed to be rubbed, massaged and stroked to the boiling point.

Jake chuckled, enjoying the effect his hand had on his girlfriend's cunt. He kept stroking up and down the girl's pussy, hoping Jennifer wouldn't realize that he didn't know what or where a clit was. He wanted to make her feel as good as she made him feel when she jacked him off. He must have been doing something right, he thought. She hadn't ever turned down a date with him. Now, with her panties down around her ankles, she was obviously having a good time. Jake slid his fingers to her cunthole and began pushing two of them inside.

Jennifer gasped. Her tight pussy began stretching to take the fingers. Her cunt cream flowed even more heavily to help ease the way. Spreading her legs even wider, she squirmed on the car scat to suck the fingers in. The fingers worked back and forth in short, sharp thrusts. With each push, they slid deeper into the young girl's wet pussy. With each push, Jennifer's body jerked and she groaned in pleasure. Ohhhhh, how good it is, she thought. If only he'd rub my clit, it would be so much better.

Jake smiled as he watched the girl's reactions. Putting an arm around her shoulders, he slid his fingers all the way in. His cock was throbbing inside his pants as he rested his thumb at the top of the girl's cunt. Using the thumb for leverage, he began moving his two fingers in little circles, and then from side to side and in and out. He was gratified to hear the girl's sharp grunts of pleasure.

"Ohhhh, that's it, ohhhhh, oh, do it to me! Fuck me with your hand, Jake! Ohhhh, feels so good, oh, oh!"

She felt her tight cunt muscles spreading widely around the base of Jake's fingers as they dug deep. Then, as his fingers pulled back a little, her cunthole slightly closed again. She was swiftly being sent into orbit. Her body trembled as she felt the beginnings of a climax building up inside her. Almost without thinking, she wrapped one of her arms around Jake's shoulders for support. With the other, she felt in his lap for the hard lump she knew would be there.

Jake groaned, feeling her touch. "Ohhhh, yeah, baby. Touch my cock. Take it out and play with it!" He thrust his cock up against her hand for emphasis, his fingers working more energetically in her pussy.

As Jennifer began doing as she had been told, her brain began fogging over. "Don't stop, oh, don't stop! I'm-I'm gonna c-cum! Aaaahhhh, nnngggghhhh!" she gasped. Her hips gyrated, pushing her cunt hard against the boy's hand. Her clit expanded, pulsing and throbbing. Her young body trembled, about to explode in pleasure. The two fingers swiftly plunged in and out of her cunt, faster and faster as she began to cum.

Her whole body tensed. A warm gush of juices flowed out of her cunt and coated Jake's hand. She convulsed as his fingers slipped and slid in her fuckhole, while his thumb kept massaging her swollen clit. Her muscles tightened up and released with her spasms as her numbed brain was overcome by the intense pleasure. She forgot where she was or what she was doing as she came under the boy's finger-fucking hand. The breath was forced out of her lungs in a rush. Her eyes were squeezed tightly closed, and she gripped the boy tightly around the shoulders as she experienced the heights of pleasure. She had temporarily forgotten about Jake's cock, but as her orgasm began to slow down, it quickly came back to mind. She again began rubbing it through the boy's pants.

Jake pumped his fingers more slowly in the girl's cunt when he sensed that her climax had ended. As he felt her relax, he gently pulled his fingers out of her fuckhole. Wetness dripped from them, and his entire hand glistened with her cream. He held his fingers in front of the girl's face, waving them under her nose.

"Here, baby. Lick my fingers while you rub my cock," he whispered.

The powerful aroma of her own cunt wafted into her nostrils. Jennifer's brain swam in excitement. It was something Jake had asked her to do on several previous occasions, but she had always refused. Each time the suggestion had been made, she found her resolve weakening. She was now sorely tempted to do as he suggested, but she still couldn't bring herself to do the perverted act.

"N-no, Jake, I can't do that," she stammered. She began unfastening the boy's pants to take his mind off of it. As she reached inside his pants and pulled out his stiff six inches of prick, she felt a wonderful sense of power over him. She had done this to him. She had made his cock get hard. She had filled the boy with lust. It was she who had turned his cock into a rigid cylinder of throbbing steel. Never mind that he had recently done the same to her cunt. Gently, her soft hand began stroking.

"Mmmmmm, oh, yeah, Jennifer. Play with my cock, baby!" He thrust his cock up and out as the girl began jacking him off. He held his fingers under his nose and inhaled deeply, a smile on his face.

Jennifer wrapped her hand around Jake's prick. She felt its heat burning into her palm. It throbbed powerfully. Gently, she squeezed his engorged cockflesh. She began slowly pumping the boy's satiny prick skin. Jake leaned back and pulled the girl against him as the softness of her hand started working its magic. Filled with lust, he pulled her mouth to his.

Jennifer pushed her lips against her boyfriend's and opened her mouth. Her tongue snaked out and flicked over Jake's lips just as his tongue was coming out to meet hers. Their tongues met and began licking each other, softly pushing and nudging. Their heads turned from side to side, lips wetly sliding and tongues working. Still, Jennifer jerked him off.

Loving the velvet heat of the boy's cock, Jennifer pulled and stroked it. Her hand slid to his prick base and she encircled it. She pulled his loose cockflesh in short strokes, squeezing and massaging. Then her hand slipped up to the middle and began lightly rubbing. Softly slipping up to his swollen cock crown, the girl's fingers began twisting and turning and kneading his reddened prickflesh. Her fingers traced around his big pisshole. The little bit of slippery wetness seeping from his piss-slit was picked up and smeared around. Jake groaned into Jennifer's mouth as his fluids made the girl's fingers slip and slide over his cockhead. His cock pulsed harder, and his tongue began working more frantically.

Feeling like her tongue and lips were being

sucked into Jake's mouth, Jennifer expertly massaged his cock. Her hand squeezed its way back to the thick base and to his balls. Gently, she tickled the boy's ball-sac. Her fingers went under his balls and hefted them. She rolled them in her hand as she felt their weight. Then her hand flicked back to the base and squeezed and stroked once again.

She broke off the kiss to focus all her attention on the cock in her hand. She stared intently, pumping in long, slow strokes, from the base to the tip. With the other hand, she felt his balls and began playing with them at the same time. As the boy's cock swelled even bigger and harder, Jennifer's eyes shined with excitement. She loved seeing what she could do to a cock. From the way this one was swelling, she knew it would not be long before the boy spurted his cum into her hand.

Jake moaned his lust. "Honey, oh, it feels good! Damn, you do that so good, baby." His voice lowered. "But, there's something you could do to make it even better, Jennifer. Will you?" He looked at the girl, his eyes communicating his desire.

Astonished, Jennifer looked up. She had already made it clear to him that he could not fuck her. That was for marriage. However, she did like the boy. She wondered bow she could make it better for him without putting it in her cunt. Warily, she asked, "How can I do that?"

Hesitating, Jake whispered, "Put your mouth on it." He stroked her soft hair.

Jennifer recoiled in shock. Put her mouth on it! The thought of his slimy cum spurting into her mouth filled her with revulsion. "W-what? No! No I won't do it! I don't want that stuff in my mouth!" she cried, indignantly.

"But baby, please. It'll feel so much better. I've heard a lot about it. Lots of people do it, honey. Please, I-I'll tell you when I'm about to cum, and you can pull your head away," he begged.

"No! I don't care how many people do it. I'm not going to. Besides, how do I know you'll tell me when you're gonna cum?"

"I'll tell you, I promise I will! You can pull your mouth off it then. Please, Jennifer. Suck my cock!" He pushed her head down toward his throbbing cock, like he had done many times in his dreams. In the dreams, the girl had hungrily opened her mouth and started sucking him. She hadn't even slowed down when he came, and she eagerly sucked and slurped his cream. But in cold reality, it was not to be. Jennifer resisted his push with a shake of her head.

"No, Jake! Ooooooh!" She tossed her head with a snap, grimacing in disgust. "I'm not gonna put your cock in my mouth. You're just gonna have to be happy with this." She squeezed his cock and resumed jacking him off, an odd look on her face. Jake sat back in defeat, consoling himself with the thought that at least the seed had been planted in the girl's mind.

He soon got over it as his cock registered the wondrous effects of Jennifer's hand. He had to admit that she pumped him expertly. His cock kept engorging until he thought it would burst and spray them with blood. Damn, it did feel good.

Jennifer thrilled as she watched the boy's cock getting harder in her grasp. She began massaging faster and harder as she sensed the boy's climax was near. She cupped his balls, feeling them tightening up in preparation.

Jake stroked the girl's hair and neck as his load boiled up from his balls. His body started trembling with the force of his unleashed passion. Relief was on the way. "Aaaahhhh, baby, jack me off! Do it, nnnmmmggghhh, oooohhhh, yeah, don't stop! I'm-I'm gonna c-cum! Oh-uhhhh!"

Jennifer's pussy was creaming as she pumped in long, hard strokes, squeezing and pulling the stiff cock flesh. She massaged the boy's balls in gentle circles as Jake began gyrating his ass. She felt him wildly caressing her head and neck as he went out of his mind with pleasure. Damn, it excited her so much to have him so under her power! She could feel the powerful preliminary spasms as he was about to cum. Quickly taking her hand away from his balls, she cupped it under the boy's cockhead to catch his load.

Jake gasped, his whole body quivering. "H-here I cum! Ohhhh, aaarrrggghhh!" He grunted and held his breath as his cock exploded in a thick stream of cum. The breath was slowly pressed out of his lungs as his muscles tensed and his toes curled up.

"Oh!" panted Jennifer. As she watched closely, her hand swiftly pumping, the boy's cock convulsed. The hot, wet cum flooded out of his pisshole and into her waiting palm. The first powerful squirt almost shot over her hand. Some of it dripped over the side. As she kept up her long stroking, the boy's cum spurted and spurted into her palm. She watched, wide-eyed and breathing hard. The thick, wet, warm white wads of cum made a deep puddle in her palm as she wrung the boy's cock dry. When Jake slumped back into the seat, the girl pumped slower, still milking it of every last drop.

Jennifer's cunt was now gushing. She was ready for Jake to finger-fuck her pussy again. She lifted her mouth to his for a wet kiss, and froze.

At that moment, one of the school's vice principals pounded on the window and ordered them out of the car.

CHAPTER 2

Jake gave a start and looked around wildly. He spied the vice-principal for boys, Mr. Hawthorne, staring at him. He was acutely aware of his own cum-dripping cock.

"Ya'll clean yourselves up and come to my office." He turned and headed for his office in long, determined strides.

"Awwwww, fuck!" wailed Jake. "Goddamn that son of a bitch!"

"That bastard!" cried Jennifer, at the same time. Her heart was racing. She trembled nervously as she got out some tissues with one hand while gingerly cupping Jake's cum in the other. Quickly, she dabbed up the sticky mess, while Jake wiped off his cock, then put it back into his pants.

Damn it, she had told Jake it was too risky to sit out in his car in the school parking lot. Finals began tomorrow, and they could be expelled. Fuck!

Her body was shaken by tremors of fear as she thought of having to explain to her parents. She couldn't bear the thought of having to take the whole semester over again. It would be quite a setback, not to mention being a severe embarrassment.

Jake was babbling, "Let's deny it! We'll say we were just sitting here. We weren't doing anything! We're innocent!"

"Now come on, Jake. It's no use. Nobody'll believe us. Nobody in this whole fucking world'll take our word over his." She dejectedly pulled up her panties and straightened her dress.

"B-but, Jennifer! We can't just go in there and admit the truth! We'll be kicked out of school. You know how that asshole gets his kicks. The more people he can expel from school, the better he likes it. We gotta deny it!" he pleaded. Jennifer opened her door.

"No, goddamn it. I told you. We'll just have to face up to it and hope they won't do anything to us." She swallowed hard and got out.

Jake whined the whole way to the office, trying to get her to change her mind. It was no use. Jennifer was raised as a good girl. Her parents had always told her to tell the truth. It simply was not in her to lie, even if it would save her skin.

Larry Hawthorne, the boy's vice-principal,

stood in the door to his office, waiting for them. He was a tall man, almost twice their ages. He had thick black hair, and eyes to match. When he walked, his big chest was usually thrust out. Sometimes, when his shirt was unbuttoned, you could see a bit of black hair poking out. He had one hell of a mean reputation around the school. Jake took one look at Hawthorne's stance and his knees turned to jelly.

"Come in, Jake," said Hawthorne. His face was an unreadable mask as he spoke, but his eyes were shining. Quaking, Jake slid past the man and into the well-furnished office.

Jennifer watched Jake, contempt on her face. She turned blankly to Hawthorne, realizing that he was speaking to her. Her look turned defiant. She was determined to take whatever might come, and not to buckle under the pressure. She was ready to take full responsibility for her actions, no matter what.

Hawthorne's gaze roved up and down the girl's body. He very much liked what he saw. She was petite, slender and fine boned. She was a little over five feet tall, and around one hundred pounds. She was innocent and young, and could easily have passed for several years younger than she was.

Her hair was parted on the left. It was light brown and long, ending in soft, dainty curls. Her open blue eyes were cat-like, wide and narrow. Her eyebrows were dark, slim and perfectly shaped. Her nose was small and delicately chiseled. Her mouth was slightly downturned at the corners, and her lips looked soft and red. Her teeth were small and white. After lingering over her mouth, the man's gaze traveled farther down the girl's fine body.

Her perky tits were thrust up and out against the top of her thin dress. She wore no bra, and her nipples pointed through the material. The man stared hard at the smooth valley between them, wishing her dress were cut just a little lower. Her slim waist was clearly outlined by the narrow belt that pulled in her dress. The dress smoothly curved out again to follow the gentle flaring of her hips. The dress stopped just above her knees. From what Hawthorne could see of her legs, they were firm and velvet smooth. The flawless, creamy white flesh that he could see called out to him. As his cock started to rise, he wanted to fall to his knees and worship her body.

Instead, he said, "Mrs. Johanson's waiting for you. Go see her." Noticing the way the girl was looking at him, he added, "You're in trouble, honey."

Jennifer turned haughtily and began walking down to the next office. Her head was held high.

Hawthorne eyeballed the girl's firm ass as she shook it from side to side. No one noticed the fleeting grin that passed across his face as he stared hard, then went into his office.

Jennifer went into Mrs. Johanson's office and found the vice-principal for girls sitting behind her desk, waiting for her. The woman looked up as Jennifer entered and closed the door behind her. The girl gulped, losing some of her determination as she saw the lady staring it her.

Mary Johanson was at least ten years older than the girl, and maybe more. She was a little taller than Jennifer. Her large, expressive brown eyes were complemented by her short, wavy auburn hair. She had a large, wide mouth with full lips. Her face was smooth and untroubled, yet there was something menacing about her that Jennifer could feel. As the woman sat behind her desk, Jennifer could see part of her tanned chest and a bit of pure white cleavage between her great tits. The woman sensed Jennifer's fear and smiled with her lips, but not with her eyes. It only served to increase Jennifer's discomfort.

"H-hello, Mrs. Johanson," Jennifer said, almost whispering. "I guess you know why I'm here."

The woman looked her up and down before answering, taking in every feature of the young girl's fine body. "Yes. Yes, I do." She leaned back, her voice hardening as she said, "Now, explain yourself."

"Well it's-it's kind of embarrassing, Mrs. Johanson. You see, my boyfriend and I-we-" her voice trailed off. Beginning again, she said, "Well we were sitting in his car, and-" She stopped, at a lost for words.

Now she was realizing how incriminating her story would sound.

Mrs. Johanson stood up and came around the desk. She said, "I understand, Jennifer. You pulled down your panties and let him play with your cunt." Jennifer was shocked. "Then you pulled out his stiff prick. Or maybe it was the other way around." Her gaze slithered up and down Jennifer's body again. "Hmmmmm, you do look like the kind of young bitch who would grab at a boy's cock, don't you." It was a statement, not a question.

Jennifer gasped. "Ma'am, since you already know what we were doing, can we please get this over with?"

"Quiet! I'm doing the talking here." When Jennifer stood there open-mouthed, the woman continued. "As I was saying before you interrupted me. Regardless of what order things occurred in, you pulled out the boy's cock. You jacked him off until his cum spurted in your hand. What did you do with the cum after Mr. Hawthorne caught you?

Did you lick it up and swallow it? Answer me!" Red-faced, the girl began sobbing, "No, I didn't lick it up. Why are you doing this to me? Just punish me and get it over with please." The woman sneered. "You little sluts are all alike." Then she patted down her dress. "All right, since you want to get it over with, we can. Let's see-I could expel you from school for this. Then all your work this semester would have been wasted." She looked hard at the girl. Receiving the appropriate amount of cringe, she continued. "Or you could submit to my own special brand of punishment and stay in school." She sniffed, nodding her head up and down. Her eyes bored holes in the girl the whole time.

"W-what is it? Oh, Mrs. Johanson, I do want to stay in school? Please, tell me what it is!"

The woman's gaze again darted up arid down the girl's curvaceous body. She said, "All right, but before I do, there s one more thing I could do-suspension for five days. However, since finals are this week, it would be the same as expelling you." She looked at the girl as if waiting for a response.

Jennifer couldn't keep the ray of hope from sounding in her voice. She eagerly cried, "Okay, okay. Punish me. I really don't have much choice, do I? Please, just don't kick me out of school, Mrs. Johanson. Anything but that!"

The woman nodded, knowing the girl was hers. "Okay, Jennifer. We're gonna do it my way." She smiled. "I'm glad you're being sensible." After a moment's hesitation, she told the girl, "Now, what you need is a good spanking, and I'm gonna give it to you. Pull down your panties and lean across my desk."

Jennifer stepped back, surprise registering on her pretty face. She needed another moment to think. In her mind, she replayed the alternatives. Trembling, she thought of exposing herself to the older woman. After arguing with herself for a split second, she knew there was only one thing she could do.

Taking a deep breath, she slowly said, "Okay, Mrs. Johanson. I'll do it." She began raising her dress.

Watching closely, the woman said, "One more thing, Jennifer. From now on, you are to do exactly as I tell you. Do not speak again unless I ask you a question. Don't make any noise or protest. I won't hurt you. Is that understood?"

"Yes, Ma'am," whispered Jennifer, her voice so low that it could hardly be heard. Again, she began raising her dress to get at her panties.

Mrs. Johanson's glance flicked over the young girl's tits. Then her gaze roved down slowly, until she got to the girl's feet. Her gaze slithered over

Jennifer's smooth, creamy legs until she got to the slowly raising hemline of the dress. As the dress rose, her gaze rose with it.

Jennifer uncomfortably noticed the woman's gaze and she trembled. She was getting lusty signals, and thought she must be wrong. It was impossible for the older woman to be sexually attracted to her. Why, the respected vice principal had been at the school for as long as she could remember. She shook her head to clear her mind, then hooked her fingers into her panties; She yanked them down to her ankles, bending over as she did so. There was nothing she could do about her wildly beating heart.

The woman said, "That's fine, honey. Now, lie across my desk and flip your dress up onto your back. I don't want it getting in the way."

"Yes, Ma'am," Jennifer stammered. She bobbled a couple of steps to the big oak desk; With a grunt, she bent across it. Her face flushed, she slipped up the back of her dress.

Mary Johanson suppressed a sharp gasp. With her hind around her throat, she stared with rapidly glazing eyes at the young girl's upturned ass. The girl's satiny smooth asscheeks were firm and round. There was a deep crack between her beautiful asscheeks. The woman could not keep from staring up and down the young girl's legs and ass. Her breath came quicker. She knew she had never seen such a fine, firm ass. The girl's tender white flesh glowed with freshness and health, from her pretty feet and slender legs, all the way up to her flawless, creamy asscheeks.

Jennifer lay there, silently waiting for the slap she knew would be coming. The cool air caressed her ass, and she felt tingles of sensation coming from the area. She was still hot and unsatisfied from her rudely interrupted session with Jake. With a start, she realized she was excited by the strange turn of events. She closed her eyes.

Chills raced up and down her spine as-she felt the cool touch of the lady's hand on her ass. The hand lightly cupped her asscheeks and rubbed them up and down. Then she felt a light slapping, first on one cheek and then on the other. Reflexively, her asscheeks began tensing for the swats she knew to be forthcoming. She braced herself, and just in time. The older woman brought her hand far back, then swung.

With a resounding smack, flesh met flesh. Jennifer's body jerked with the sudden jolt. A stinging pain rippled out from her ass. Before her asscheeks had stopped quivering, the next blow landed. This time, Jennifer couldn't keep from grunting. She gripped the edge of the desk and willed herself not to cry out as the woman's hand met her ass for the third time. Her brain filling up with pain, she felt her asscheeks getting hotter as they swelled with blood and turned crimson. She began to moan.

Mrs. Johanson was enjoying herself. She had always known she had a dominant side, but it wasn't until she came to the school as vice principal that she had realized how much it turned her on to demonstrate her power. It was surprising to find out which of the girls enjoyed her treatment, and how many there were! Each time she found a new one, she became more excited than she had the last time.

This time was no different. As soon as she had seen Jennifer, she had suspected that the girl had a deep submissive streak running through her very core. She had known right then that the girl would make an interesting subject. The girl didn't know herself well enough to realize her need to be dominated, but Mrs. Johanson would take care of that. She would take control of the girl, making sure Jennifer quickly found out about herself and enjoyed every minute of it. Jennifer would be broken in properly, like a good girl should. Mrs. Johanson kept swinging, thrilling with each sudden slap against the girl's soft asscheeks.

Jennifer lay across the desk, her face twisted in a grimace of pain. The pain shooting out from her ass -had steadily taken over her brain until it now overshadowed any other thoughts she might have had. The only thing she knew was pain as her soft asscheeks were repeatedly beaten. Biting her lip, she tried to stifle her moans.

Suddenly, the beating stopped. Jennifer put her head on her arms and lay still. Her ass was on fire, quivering and tingling in shock. Her legs shook as she held onto the desk to keep from sliding off. Gradually, her breathing slowed. Even though her ass burned, she was grateful that it hadn't been worse. As the pain began to subside, she realized with a shock that her cunt was gushing. She could feel the hot juices dripping down her thighs in a steady, Wet stream. For an instant, she forgot about the older woman, but then it came to her that the woman had a clear, unobstructed view between her legs. She tried to close them together as she began straightening up. A hand on her back held her down.

"Be still!" commanded Mrs. Johanson. "Don't get up 'til I tell you to, Jennifer." She placed her other hand on the girl's ass, gently stroking. "Now, just relax. I'm going to massage your ass so it won't be bruised in the morning.

Jennifer stiffened as she felt the woman's hand caressing her ass. As she lay helplessly pinned, a strange sensation began coming over her. She felt

Mrs. Johanson gently rubbing up and down her warm asscheeks. The woman 's soft hand glided up her ass, then slid down to cup her tender, sensitive assflesh. Pressing more firmly, Mrs. Johanson began massaging in a strong, circular motion. First one cheek, and then the other began tingling in a totally new manner. Jennifer gradually relaxed and began to enjoy it. The hand began gliding back and forth from cheek to cheek, lightly dipping into the crack between them each time it crossed.

Mrs. Johanson knew she had Jennifer hooked as soon as the girl's body relaxed under her touch. She stared hard in between Jennifer's asscheeks as she rubbed them. Each time her hand switched to Jennifer's other asscheek and dipped into the girl's asscrack, she applied enough pressure to open up the girl's ass and expose her asshole. Jennifer's anus looked so soft and tender. Seeing and smelling the young girl's cuntjuices running down between her thighs made the woman want to drop to her knees and lick it up. Filling with lust, she could hardly hold herself back. If she didn't eat Jennifer's tender pussy this time, she would be sure to do so the next time, she vowed.

Jennifer could feel the air caressing her asshole each time the older woman spread her anus open. She was delightfully aware of her burning, itching cunt. The aroma of her own pussy was so overpowering that it completely filled her nostrils. She was ashamed of herself for being so turned on. Still, her pussy tingled with unfulfilled desire as the woman's hand fondled her reddened asscheeks. She had to admit that it felt good. Damn good. The massage continued, and Jennifer found herself wishing for something more.

Mrs. Johanson knew that the girl was extremely aroused. She knew from experience how good an ass massage felt. She was delighted to hear a groan escape the girl's lips. It was time to make her move.

Jennifer's whole body was tingling with life. She wanted to be rubbed, stroked, caressed. The fire of lust was inside her, and there was only one way to quench it. She had to go home and frig herself until she came. Before she could move, however, she felt the lady's hand sliding between her asscheeks. It was unexpected, but felt so good that she could not suppress a sigh of pleasure.

Fingers lightly traced their way into her asscrack, and then began sliding down toward her asshole. Jennifer felt herself trembling in anticipation. Involuntarily, her asshole twitched as the woman's fingers neared it. As Mrs. Johanson reached her anus, however, she began circling around her asshole instead of touching it. Her fingers delicately slid around the girl's puckered asshole in a gentle, but firm massage. Now Jennifer desperately wanted the fingers to rub her asshole. But they didn't. After a few light trips around her brown slit hole, they resumed their downward journey.

The fingers neared Jennifer's cunt. Jennifer arched her back, waiting for the caress. Instead of touching her pussy, they went on down around her cuntlips to her wet inner thighs. Picking up the slick juices, Mrs. Johanson's fingers effortlessly slid up and down in a wonderful massage. After tickling both inner thighs, they began heading back up to the grits cunt.

This time they went straight tot Jennifer's pussylips. Jennifer was almost ready to beg for it, when the woman's hand began cupping her cunt. The swollen flesh sent signals of extreme lust to her brain's the woman's hand rubbed and massaged. Her reverie was interrupted by the sound of the woman's voice. "How do you feel, Jennifer?" whispered Mrs. Johanson.

"Mmmmmm, oh, good," moaned the girl. She couldn't help herself. She was hotter than she had ever been before. She wanted to cum, and badly.

"Spread your legs," the woman said.

Jennifer hardly hesitated to do as she was told. At first, she had been ashamed of herself, but not any longer. She was hot and horny, and her pussy needed attention. Mrs. Johanson was providing that attention, and that was all she asked. It felt wonderful. She spread her legs as far apart as she could.

The woman's wonderful fingers dove between her pussylips. They slid into her cuntslit and began flicking up and down, smearing her cream all over. They slid to her fuckhole and began circling the swollen rim, gradually swirling inside. First the tip of one finger slid inside her. It began thrusting in and out, sliding deeper with each thrust. With the aid of the girl's slippery cuntjuices, the woman's finger swiftly buried itself all the way in. Jennifer grunted in happiness.

The finger pumped several times before pulling out and slowly rubbing down her cuntslit to her clit. It flicked over her cunt, and then began circling around it. The lone finger was soon joined by others, and together they began massaging the entire area around Jennifer's cunt. Jennifer gripped the edge of the desk harder. Her breathing came faster. Her brain was clouding over with a fever she had never known.

Knowing the girl was now completely in her power, Mrs. Johanson slid her foot under her desk. Feeling the small red button, she pressed it. Seconds later, a panel slid back in the wall separating her office from Hawthorne's.

CHAPTER 3

Silently, Hawthorne crept in and noiselessly slid the panel shut. Careful to make no sound, he began unfastening his pants.

Jennifer was blissfully unaware of anything around her except the woman's soft hand rubbing her clit. Her eyes were closed as she was sent into dreamland. Her lips were slightly parted, and she panted in lust. A cry of joy shot from her mouth as she felt fingers pushing into her cunt while the hand kept rubbing her clit. Fingers pushed and probed her wet cunthole, then were withdrawn. She could feel her climax building up as the pleasure waves spread throughout her body.

Mrs. Johanson's hands were busy on Jennifer's cunt as she motioned for Hawthorne to move closer. With his huge cock straining out, Hawthorne got behind the girl. He wanted so badly to fuck her. He stared lustfully as the woman's hands roved between the girl's slender legs. The lady's fingers slid over Jennifer's cuntlips, lightly traced around and over her asshole, then Went back to her cunt. Her eyes shining, Johanson firmly opened Jennifer's tight pussylips. Silently cautioning Hawthorne to be quiet, she signaled him to put his cock inside the girl. Hawthorne stared for a moment at Jennifer's bright-pink, glistening inner cuntflesh. His heart was racing as his throbbing cock neared her gaping fuckhole.

Jennifer moaned louder as her pussylips were pulled wide apart. Her tight cunt gaped open. She could feel the air blowing into her fuckhole. Something big, hot and hard pressed between her legs. After sliding up and down her cuntslit, it pushed between her cuntlips and centered on her fuckhole. While Mrs. Johanson kept frigging, Jennifer's juicy cunthole began stretching. Her pussy slowly opened up as the big thing exerted more and more pressure.

The girl wondered what the woman was using on her cunt. She assumed it was a dildo. She had never used one, but if she had known it would feel this good, she certainly would have.

"Ohhhhh, yeahhhh, Mrs. Johanson. Oh! It's good-mmmnnn, ahhhh, ah, oh, yeah!" she moaned. Her ass began moving against the hand and the big thing pushing into her pussy.

The woman frigged Jennifer's cunt harder and faster. With her thumbs, she held the girl's pussy spread. Jennifer's pink fuckhole yawned open to allow Hawthorne to put his cock in. The man and the woman smiled at each other, while the girl lay across the desk with an expression of total ecstasy on her face. Hawthorne carefully stroked his cock back and forth in short thrusts to let the girl's cream spread over his prickhead. Goddamn, her pussy was so fucking tight!

Jennifer groaned. The wonderful fingers slid wound her cunt. They fucked over her fucknub, stroking it back and forth. They circled it, gently massaging. They pressed firmly and rubbed the whole area around it. All the while, she felt her young cunt stretching wider as the big, hot thing pushing against her pussy pushed harder. The big thing pumped in quick, short thrusts. It steadily eased deeper between her swollen cuntlips with each stroke. Jennifer experienced a wonderful, warm feeling spreading throughout her young body. Her tight pussy had never before been stretched so much. The big thing kept pushing, forcing her tiny fuckhole to expand to take it.

"Ohhhh! Ohhhh, it-it hurts. Ohhhh, please, please! You're stretching me! Nnnngggghhh!" she grunted.

All she got in response was a low chuckle. The stiff thing kept pushing, stretching her cunt wider. She gasped in part pain, part pleasure. Just as she felt she would be torn in two, the stretching stopped and the thing slid deeply into her cunt. She gasped in sudden pleasure. The inner walls of her cunt tightly gripped the big thing. It was enough to send her over the brink. She shoved back against it.

"Ohhhhh, ooooo! I'm gonna-cum I"

Her smooth body jerked on the desk. Her eyes screwed shut, and her lips were parted. She panted. She sobbed and moaned. Her cunt swelled and throbbed under the vice-principal's expert caress. Waves of electric climax raced up and down her body. Her cunt squeezed tightly around the hard thing inside it. She came harder than she ever had in her life. All her muscles tensed and released in powerful spasms that took over her brain and turned her into a mindless servant of lust. It was almost too much for her to bear as her brain fogged over with sheer delight. Her orgasm seemed to go on forever before she slowly began returning to the world around her.

Panting, she exclaimed, "Oh, that was good! Uhhhhh, oh, yeah, so good. Fuck, I feel better. Thanks."

The woman replied, "My pleasure, Jennifer."

She stopped rubbing the young girl's cunt, winking at Larry as she did so. Jennifer stayed in position, waiting for the hard thing to be taken out of her cunt. As she waited, her pussy still burning, she turned to look. With a start, she recognized Mr. Hawthorne.

Her voice climbing, she shrieked, "Wh-what's going on? Ohhhhh!"

Clawing at the desk, the realization dawned on her that she was being fucked.

It seemed the horny pair were going to make her do whatever they wanted, and there was nothing she could do about it.

Hawthorne chuckled, "What's the matter, Jennifer? You afraid to get a cock in your cunt? A little while ago, you were jerking off your boyfriend." He again gently stroked his cock in and out of hers fuckhole. "Too late now, honey. Half my cock's already in your cunt, and the rest is fixin' to follow. This is gonna be the best thing you ever had. Now get ready for it, 'cause here it comes." He held onto her waist above the flare of her hips. While Mrs. Johanson helped hold the girl down, Hawthorne fucked more of his cock into her.

Jennifer was scarlet with the humiliation of it all. The prize she had been saving for her future husband had been taken away from her. Though suffering from the degradation, she couldn't keep from moaning as her cunt opened up for his big cock.

Finally, she faced the fact that her cunt was getting fucked, and that she might as well settle back to enjoy it.

Her pussy opened wider. The man's cock went deeper than anything ever had before. The short, gentle strokes began getting to her. Each time, his prick edged a little deeper into her slick pussy. She could feel her cunt throbbing, and before she knew it, the pleasure began building inside her.

Hawthorne sensed the girl's change of heart. He eased his cock deeper with each thrust, marveling at the tightness of her cunt. It was so wet, so hot, so wonderful! He looked down to see Jennifer's pussylips spread widely with his cock splitting them apart. The sight made his head swim with excitement. His cock throbbed inside her fuckhole, and he knew that it wouldn't take too much more to make him cum. Growing more excited, he began fucking his cock in faster. He wanted it all the way inside the girl's soft pussy before he shot his load inside her.

Jennifer felt great. As her pussy split apart, she was filled with pleasure. She squeezed her cunt muscles around his cock as it slid deeper. She suddenly realized that she wanted his big cock as deep as it could go up her cunt. Her ass moved in circles, and she loved the stretching feeling she got out of it as his cock stirred up the tender flesh inside her pussy.

Hawthorne's hand softly gripped the girl's waist as he prepared to bury his cock to the ball. A couple inches were still in the open air, and he was ready to slip them in. Pulling back a few more inches, he held the girl more tightly. Firmly, he fucked his cock all the way into her cunt. With a groan of happiness, he ground powerfully against her ass.

Jennifer's muffled grunt was heard as she was jolted by the man's pumping. She gasped as the soft flesh of her pussy yielded under the powerful onslaught. She moaned as she felt his big prick digging all the way inside her cunt. She grunted with swiftly building pleasure as she felt the man grinding against her ass, fucking her hard and deep.

"Mmmmppphhhh! G-gooood! Ohhhh, yeah," she groaned. She could feel her cunt swelling and dripping pussyjuice. Her cunt was throbbing, and thrills ran through her young body as she was wonderfully fucked for the first time.

Almost without realizing what she was doing, she ground back at the man fucking her. Each time his big cock fucked into her cunthole, she pushed back hard. She squeezed the man's prick with her tight cunt muscles, grinding back with her ass and moaning in happiness. Each time his cock pulled back, she felt her fuckhole contracting as it emptied.

Breathlessly, she waited, with her pussy dripping in anticipation, for the next deep stroke. When it came, she gratefully moaned as she ground hard against Hawthorne once again.

Both the man and the woman were pleased at Jennifer's swift change of attitude. Hawthorne fucked harder, while Johanson stopped holding the girl down. Johanson watched the man fucking into Jennifer's soft cunt, plain envy apparent in her eyes. Her own cunt was dripping juices down her thighs. Her breath was coming faster than before, and she was horny as hell. She turned back to the young girl across her desk and began stroking her firm body through her dress.

Jennifer's eyes were glazing over as she felt the woman's hands running through her hair and down the back of her neck. Tingles vibrated out from the areas the woman touched. The woman rubbed lower down and massaged Jennifer's back between her shoulder blades. Then she used both hands to stroke the girl's soft hips. After massaging briefly, she felt underneath to the girl's firm belly. Slowly, her hands slid up to the young girl's tits. They circled and stroked Jennifer's tender titflesh, and Jennifer could hold back her moans no longer. "Ohhhhh, Mrs. Johanson, it feels good! Ohhhhh, ahhhh, mmmm!" Her whole body was quivering with lust. She had never experienced anything so good in her whole life. Still panting, she fucked back against Hawthorne's digging, fucking cock. She was taking it all and begging for more as she was fucked out of her young mind by the man's swollen prick.

Mrs. Johanson, growing feverish to caress the girl's naked flesh, said, "Larry, stop for a minute, will you? I want to take off her dress." Larry reluctantly stopped fucking, slamming his cock as deeply as possible, then holding it there. The girl's wet, warm cunt tightly enveloped his cock. Mrs. Johanson quickly unfastened Jennifer's dress and yanked it off, then pushed the girl back down across the desk. As soon as it was off, Larry started fucking the girl's tight pussy again.

Jennifer thrilled as she was totally exposed to the two vice-principals. She now felt the full heat of Larry's body as he lay partly on her ass and partly on her back while he fucked her. She thrilled at the feel of the woman's hands on her bare tit mounds. After rubbing them in circles and squeezing gently, the woman began pinching Jennifer's nipples in between her fingers. Jennifer moaned her appreciation as her nipples were pinched and pulled. The woman was pinching them at the base, then pulling them out long and slow. Jennifer could feel her nipples stretching out and enlarging in excite-ment. She kept grinding her ass onto Hawthorne's stomach as they fucked themselves into a frenzy of lust.

"Yeah, Jennifer. That's the way to do it. Fuck me, baby. Fuck me with that tight pussy of yours. Ahhhhh, uuuhhhhh," moaned Hawthorne.

"Ohhh! Oh! Ohhhh, ahhhh, ooohhhh, yes!" panted Jennifer. Urged on by the man's words, she worked her cunt more vigorously.

Mrs. Johanson put her head close to Jennifer's and whispered, "Kiss me, Jennifer!" Her mouth moved toward the girl's.

Jennifer opened her eyes and peered at the woman's unlined face. As her cunt and clit swelled with the steady fucking, her normal inhibitions were forgotten. When she felt the woman's soft mouth pressing against hers, she didn't object. Instead, her lips parted and her tongue flicked out to taste the other woman's mouth. When the lady's tongue flicked out to meet hers, she licked and sucked at it. To her surprise, it was hardly different than kissing a man. If anything, it was even more exciting in its perversity. Her mouth slid wetly over Johanson's as the girls got hotter over each other.

Jennifer could feel her cunt swelling larger than before. Her pussy was steadily gushing slippery cream as the man's big cock pumped in and out. With her mouth covered by Mary's, the girl could feel herself starting to cum. She began fucking back like a wild woman, opening her legs and cunt to take in the big cock, then clamping down tightly as it pulled out. Her ass shook from side to side, meeting the man's every deep thrust and trying to get more. Her lips kissed and sucked at the other woman's mouth. Johanson's hands squeezed and pulled her soft tits. She wanted to cum so badly. Even as she thought it, she could feel her body tensing until she exploded in climax.

The sounds muffled, she gasped, "Oh, ah, ah, mmmpphhh!"

Uncontrollably, she ground hard against Hawthorne. Her cunt wildly spasmed, wringing the man's cock in its warm, slippery grip. Her body jerked on the desk. She held onto the desk with all her strength as her muscles convulsed. She pressed her mouth harder against Mary's. All she was conscious of, was her rapidly splitting and closing cuntlips as the man fucked into her again and again.

Just as she began to go limp, she heard the man's cry of desire. He redoubled his fucking, slamming and grinding into the young girl's cunt even harder.

"Ohhhh, baby! Oh, mmmmm, I'm gonna, shoot cum in your cunt! Yeah, oh, yeah, work that pussy, bitch! I'm gonna cum!" He grip-ped her tightly around the waist and fucked her hard and deep. His cock swelled, and then powerful spasms wracked his body. Great, hot spurts of cum spurted into the young girl's squeezing, milking cunt. "Ohhhh, fuck! Nnnnggghh, aaannnnnggh!"

Jennifer felt the man's grip tighten. She was thrilled as she felt him fucking her like a wild animal. She braced herself against the furious onslaught. Breathing hard, she worked her cunt as she had been told and met his every thrust with her willing pussy. She felt his cock expanding, growing harder. She felt the powerful spasms running its full length as the hot cum gushed out of his swollen cockhead and splashed into her cunt. The slippery stuff made the man's cock slip and slide even better than before as it mixed with her cuntjuices.

Finally, the man slowed down and slumped onto the girl's back. Jennifer relaxed, enjoying the warmth of his body on hers. She twitched her cunt and gently pushed back at him to get every last ounce of pleasure she could get. Oh, goddamn, it was better than she had thought possible. What a mistake it had been to wait for a fuck as long as she had.

Much to her disappointment, she felt her cunt emptying of the satisfying fullness that had made her feel so good. Slowly, the man pulled his cock from the tight confines of the girl's pussy. As his prickmeat withdrew, a trickle of cum leaked out of Jennifer's cunt. It dripped down her inner thighs. Pleasure radiated from between her legs, and she gave a happy moan. She had been well-fucked today.

As Jennifer felt Mary pulling away from her, too, she was saddened that the pleasure could not last forever. Before, she had felt so comfortable, so secure. Now, she once again felt vulnerable, exposed, no longer wrapped in their warm, loving embraces. She lifted her head and turned to look at the man who had just finished fucking her.

"Oh!" she gasped. Her hand flew to her mouth as she stared at his huge, dangling cock. The fucker was about eight inches long, much bigger than her boyfriend's. It was still partially swollen and reddened. She could see her slick cunt cream coating his prick, and a bit of sticky cum dripped from his cocktip. After staring at his prick for a long moment, she gazed into the man's dark eyes. He, in turn, looked deep into hers, making her body tremble with a burning desire she had never known or felt before.

Mrs. Johanson came and put her arms around her, saying, "Jennifer, now I want you to clean up his cock." She patted the girl's head. Helping her to her feet, the woman gave Jennifer a push in the right direction.

Her face flushing, Jennifer asked, "Wh-what do I clean it with, Ma'am?"

"Your mouth."

CHAPTER 4

"What?" Jennifer looked around, bewildered. Her legs turned to jelly as she thought of putting the man's sticky, cum smeared cock in her mouth. Before she could say another word, however, Mrs. Johanson grabbed her shoulders and began forcing her to her knees.

"You heard me. I said lick his cock clean." She pushed Jennifer farther down. "Listen, bitch. I've already I old you once that you are to obey me instantly." Holding Jennifer down with one hand, the woman slapped the girl hard on the ass. "Now, do it!"

"Ouch! Stop it, I'll do it!" Jennifer yelped. She was pinned down, her feeble resistance evaporating under the lady's strong grip. Hawthorne came closer, positioning his cock near her mouth.

Jennifer looked shamefully at the man's hanging cock as it came closer to her face. Her ass stung. She could hardly mole as the woman held her in a kneeling position. She didn't want to put his dirty, sticky prick in her mouth. Her mind quickly ran over the alternatives once again, and she knew she had no choice. She consoled herself with the thought that it would soon be over and she would be allowed to go home.

She looked up with frightened, innocent eyes to see the man peering down to her. Even as she looked, the man edged closer. His cock touched her lips. She sniffed the powerful aroma of cock and cunt wafting into her nostrils. It smelled strange, but somehow it was good. She inhaled more deeply. The smell began exciting her. There was something strangely welcoming about it.

"C'mon, baby. Open your mouth," coaxed Hawthorne. He pushed his cock a little more firmly against Jennifer's mouth.

Jennifer looked into his eyes. After only a moment's hesitation, she opened her mouth. The man's warm cock slipped between her lips. The girl touched his prick with her tongue. She marveled at the silky smooth texture. The taste was unfamiliar to her, but it was not what she had expected. Like the smell, there was something strangely good about it. She stayed still, unmoving.

The man pushed all of his limp cock into her open mouth. His pubic hairs pressed against her face.

Hawthorne looked at the girl as she held his cock in her mouth. Realizing she needed instruction, he was only too willing to provide it. "Suck my cock, honey. Use your lips and tongue on it."

He placed his hands on the sides of the girl's head. Gently, he moved her head from side to side. Then he began moving her head back and forth to help her get the idea. He pulled his hips back as he pushed the girl's head away. He pushed forward with his hips as he pulled the girl's face against his body.

In response to his commands, Jennifer started sucking. Instinctively, she gripped his cock with her lips and sucked like she was drinking through a straw. Al the same time, she tried to fuck her tongue over his cockhead. She worked her tongue, feeling his limp prick flop from side to side in her mouth. As the man flicked into her mouth, her concentration was broken and her breathing was interrupted. Her head was immediately gripped tighter and pulled more roughly.

"Come on, Jennifer. I said suck it!"

Concentrating hard, Jennifer timed her breathing with the thrusts. Gradually, her lips and tongue began a coordinated effort to work on the man's cock as she got herself under control. As her head was pushed back, she wildly licked over the man's cockhead when it touched the inside of her lips. When she felt her head being pulled back down, she sucked strongly and gripped his cock firmly with her lips. The more his slick cockflesh slid in and out of her mouth, the more she found herself liking it. Even so, the only reason she sucked and licked was to please the man and keep him quiet. She didn't know how much more abuse she could take. The man began moaning his appreciation, and Jennifer knew she must be doing something right.

"Oh, yeah. That's it, you little bitch. Now you're catching on. That feels good, Jennifer. That's the way to suck cock," groaned the horny vice-principal. "Yeah, use your tongue, baby. Just keep that up and you'll get your reward pretty soon." He gyrated his hips in pleasure. His cock started getting hard again as the young girl revived it with her mouth.

The man's cock slowly slid in and out of Jennifer's mouth. Her head was being slowly twisted from side to side and pulled back and forth. As she sucked and licked, she thought she could feel his prick growing bigger. She sucked some more. Now she knew for sure that the man's cock was swelling. It stiffened more and started to fill her mouth. She began to panic. What if the man spurted cum in her mouth? She couldn't bear the thought of his slimy, gooey jizz shooting onto her tongue. She tried to pull her mouth off it, but the man's firm grip held her head still. His cock eased in and out of her lips, and as quickly as the thought of resisting crossed her mind, it vanished again.

"Lick it, Jennifer. I'm gonna pull my cock out of your mouth so you can use your lips and tongue on my prick. Lick and kiss it. Do it good, flow. He pulled back, letting his cock slide out of the young girl's open mouth.

Jennifer's eyes widened. His prick was already much bigger than it had been when she started sucking. Before she had to be told again, she quickly began licking. Upon seeing that the girl no longer had to be held, Mrs. Johanson sat back to watch.

Jennifer held onto the man's cock with one hand. Her mouth started working on his swollen prickhead. Her tongue traced its way around his cock-knob, then flicked back and forth over it. Without needing to be told, she started licking down its underside. Her tongue slid underneath his cockhead and slid toward the thick cock root. When she got there, she licked around the base. Her tongue went back up to his prickhead and again started sliding over it. She could feel the man's cock twitching under the soft, wet caress of her tongue.

Hawthorne groaned, "That's the way. You learn fast, honey. Lick up and down and all around. Lick over my piss-hole. Then lick my balls real good. After that, lick my cockhead some more and start sucking again." Lightly, his hands caressed the girl's head.

Obeying him, Jennifer started licking around the slit in his cockhead. Her tongue rapidly flicked back and forth over his pisser, and the few drops of cum seeping out of it made her tastebuds shiver with delight. Feeling his cock hardening in response to her sucking, she was filled with a sense of power. She wondered why she hadn't sucked cock before. His warm, throbbing cock felt good against her lips and tongue. She licked down the underside to the man's hairy balls.

Remembering how sensitive her boyfriend's balls were, she was careful not to lick too hard. Gently, her tongue swabbed the man's balls. She licked over his wrinkled ball-sac, feeling his big balls rolling under the pressure of her tongue. As she licked his balls, she felt his cock resting on her face. Its heat came through her smooth flesh and transmitted itself to her brain. Her brain was burning with the fever of lust. Her pussy was again dripping, and her cunt was throbbing in need.

Now the man's cock was fully engorged and straining out. Jennifer was awed by the size of his fucker as the swollen eight inches throbbed against her face. She realized it was time to suck his prick some more, and proceeded to do exactly that. She licked her way back up the underside of his cock. After swabbing his cockhead once more, tasting the cum seeping from his pisshole, she sucked it back into her mouth. It felt so fucking right to have a hot, throbbing cock in her mouth. This was what she had needed. This was what she knew she had been born to do. She had been born to suck cock.

She lovingly locked her lips around his swollen cockhead. Her tongue flicked over and over his pisshole, then rolled over and around his big cockhead. She could feel his cock pulsing as the man flexed his muscles in pleasure. Opening her mouth wider, she sucked more of the stiff prick into her mouth. Her tongue never stopped moving. She repeatedly lashed again and again over the hot prickflesh in her mouth.

Hawthorne looked at the young girl on her knees in front of him. He stared hard at her ruby lips as they gripped his cock in their wet, warm embrace. The girl looked so natural as she sucked, like she was born to it. Hawthorne could tell she was beginning to like it. From the way she now sucked and licked, it was plain to see that Jennifer's attitude about mouthing a cock had changed. The man watched more of his cock disappearing between the girl's lips. As he felt the softness of her lips and tongue, he knew he wouldn't be able to last long.

He whispered, Stroke it, and rub my balls." His hips moved as the girl's mouth kept working on his cock.

Jennifer began fondling the man's heavy balls while she sucked and licked. She squeezed his cock around the root. She hefted his balls, then gently tickled them with her fingers. The hand around his cock slowly began pumping. She sucked him, and she began jacking him off in her mouth.

Her head bobbed up and down, sliding her tightly gripping lips from the tip almost to the root of his big prick. As the man ground his hips from side to side, Jennifer moved her head to keep up. She felt him push his cock deeply into her mouth until she could take no more. She put her hand on his prick in front of her mouth and kept sucking, stroking the part she could not suck. When his cock went into her mouth, her tongue dragged along its underside. When it slid back, her lips locked around his prickhead to keep it from getting away. Her tongue swiftly licked all around his pisshole and over his cock-knob before her face went back down as far as it could once again. Soon, Jennifer noticed the man's cockhead engorging even more. His prick swelled up until it filled her mouth. The man uncontrollably fucked into her mouth. She felt his big prick swell to a hugeness she had never experienced before. It twitched and pulsed against her tongue. The man's grip grew tighter in her hair. He began pumping faster, fucking her mouth as the pleasure mounted.

"Ohhhh, Jennifer, keep sucking! You're making me cum! I'm gonna cum in your mouth, you whore! Ohhh, ahhhhh, don't-don't stop." Out of his mind with lust, he stroked her face as he fucked his cock in and out of her mouth.

Hearing the man's words, and knowing that he was about to cum in her mouth, Jennifer tried to pull her head away. She thought of the thick, sticky white jizz that was about to spurt out of the man's cock, and the thought once again almost made her stomach turn. She tried to pull back, but the man's firm grip held her head fast. Forgotten was the good taste of the cum she had already licked up. Forgotten was how right the cock had felt in her mouth. All she knew was that his cock was about to spurt jism in her mouth. She had to take her mouth off of it.

Hawthorne didn't know any of this, nor did he

care. His cock was swelling to the bursting point inside the young girl's soft, sucking mouth. The warm wetness of her sweet lips and tongue smothered and milked his cock, and he was about to cum. The pleasure was building up and he wanted to cum in her mouth. He started fucking faster. His brain clouded over. His grip grew tighter. He fucked into her mouth, pulling the girl's face against him to meet every thrust. His cock spasmed, and he gurgled, "Agggghhhh, nnnggghhh, unnnhh, oooooohhhh!"

Jennifer struggled to pull away as she felt the powerful spasming of the man's prick. Though she tried, she couldn't move her head. The man held it in an iron grip, pumping away in a mindless desire. His big cock throbbed mightily. A spasm ran its length and a flood of warm cum erupted into her mouth. Great gobs of hot cream gushed out of the slit in his cockhead and rolled over her tongue. It spurted out of his spasming cock and coated the inside of the girl's mouth.

The cum kept spurting, and his cock kept pulsing, and Jennifer couldn't help tasting his thick jizz. Her tongue recoiled as the steaming wads coated it. To her surprise and delight, the stuff tasted good. As she realized how good it was, she went at it more eagerly. Her mouth licked and sucked as the foaming cum spurted.

Now hungry for cum, Jennifer sucked and licked for all she was worth. She kept sucking and working her tongue over the man's cockhead until no more cream spurted from his empty balls. Even after she felt his grip relax on her head, she kept sucking. She held his cum in her mouth, rolling her tongue from side to side as she fully enjoyed the flavor of his slippery jizz. She kept sucking, feeling Hawthorne's cock going limp. She kept sucking until the man pushed her head away with a groan. Even as she felt her head being pushed away, she sucked strongly to get every last drop of cum.

"All right," moaned Hawthorne. "Goddamn, you milked it dry, Jennifer. You did it good."

Even as his cock pulled out of her lips, Jennifer tried to reach it again with her mouth. She lifted her face and sucked one last time on his sensitive prickhead before Hawthorne pulled it out of her reach. With a satisfied expression, the girl swished the cum around in her mouth. Sitting on her haunches, she swallowed.

Jennifer looked at the man's cock hanging limply over his big balls. She knew that she had stumbled onto something good here. It was something she wanted to repeat as often as possible from now on, she decided. Her thoughts were interrupted by Mary's fingers rubbing her cunt arid asshole. Shivers rippled throughout her feverish body.

"It's my turn now, Jennifer," the woman said.

Jennifer turned to see the woman behind her, completely naked. The lady's big tits were firm and proud, her nipples huge and circular and pink. They stood up, rubbery and swollen. Her glance slid down Mrs. Johanson's firm, sloping belly to her hairy cunt. She could see the juices dripping down the woman's thighs. Looking farther down, she looked with envy at the lady's smooth slender legs. Her heart skipped a beat as she heard the woman's next words.

"Come here, Jennifer. I said it's my turn now, I want you to eat my pussy."

CHAPTER 5

Before the girl could think, her legs began moving of their own accord. The horny woman lay down on the floor, and Jennifer crawled between her spread legs. Trembling all over, Jennifer looked at the woman's gaping fuckhole.

Beneath a furry covering of auburn hair, the woman's cunt was swollen and reddened. She had been fingering herself while watching Jennifer giving Hawthorne a blowjob. Her fuckhole was open, and Jennifer could see the bright-pink inner pussy flesh. It glistened with a thick froth of cream. The juices steadily dripped out. The whole area between the lady's legs was glistening wet. It drew the girl's face like a magnet.

Jennifer, her young lips parted, knelt down and lowered her face. As she got a closer look at Mary's cunt, she saw that her cunt was very large.

It stood out at least half an inch, throbbing with lust. Though the girl knew it was wrong, she could not stop her mouth from moving lower.

The woman put her bands on the back of Jennifer's head. She pulled the girl's face between her legs, saying, "Oh, Jennifer. Lick my pussy, honey. Suck my clit"

Jennifer inhaled the aroma of fuck-lust emanating from Johanson's cunt. It smelled like her own cuntjuices when she smelled them on Jake's fingers in the car. Her head began swimming in a sea of desire. She was disgusted at the thought of committing such an unnatural act, but she couldn't help herself. She pressed her mouth against the woman's cunt.

The warm wetness of the lady's slick pussy transmitted itself to Jennifer's lips. The girl's nose was buried in the woman's cunt hairs, and she started licking. Her tongue swiped out and licked up Johanson's smooth cuntslit. The sticky flavor of a pussy in heat tantalized her tastebuds. She licked it again, and decided that the smooth warmth of a cunt felt good against her tongue. As her initial reluctance was overcome, she started licking with more vigor.

Her tongue moved up and down between the woman's cuntlips. She lightly wiggled her tongue back and forth as she licked up to Mary's clit.

Remembering the lady's instructions to suck her clit, Jennifer covered it with her mouth. Her lips closed over Mary's swollen fucknub, and she began sucking it. In response, the woman thrust her cunt into the air and groaned at the goodness of it all.

"Oooohhh, easy, honey. Easy, suck lightly. Lick it, too," moaned Mrs. Johanson.

Jennifer eased the pressure, and started flick-ing her tongue back and forth over Mary's clit, like she had done on Hawthorne's cockhead. She gently nursed on the lady's clit, while her tongue kept working over it. She lightly flicked back and forth, then swirled her tongue around and around. Soon, the woman's moans could not be stopped.

Wanting to taste more of the woman s cream, Jennifer stopped sucking her clit. She licked back down the lady's fuck slit to her cunthole. Her tongue dipped inside. She stabbed her tongue into Mary's wet pussy, slurping up the delicious cream she found inside. She licked all around the reddened rim of the woman's cunt, loving the texture of the slick flesh against her tongue. Quickly, her tongue swirled back inside, and she began licking the lady's cunt.

Mary spread her legs wider, and drew up her knees. The feel of the girl's soft mouth got better and better. Going out of her mind with lust, she grabbed her cuntlips and pulled them wide apart to let the girl's tongue slide into her cunt even deeper.

"Ohhhh, yeahhh, ohhhh, mmmnnnnunm, ahhhh," moaned the lady. Jennifer's mouth felt so good on her pussy.

Jennifer buried heir face deeper between Mary's legs. She inhaled the strong pussy aroma, and her tongue darted in and out of the woman's spread fuckhole. Her head nodded up and down and from side to side. She then licked her way back up the lady's cuntslit to her clit. Planting her chin over Mary's open cunthole, her soft mouth opened and sucked the woman's trembling clit inside.

Her tongue swirled around Mary's fucknub, then lanced back and forth across it. Damn, it tasted good. The woman's lips jerked wildly, meeting every stab of the girl's tongue with her juicy pussy.

Suddenly, Jennifer felt herself pushed away. The woman screamed, "Ohhhhh, fuck me, Larry! Fuck me, fuck me, please!"

Jennifer quickly got out of the way. Hawthorne rushed past her and he threw himself between Mary's legs. His cock strained in the direction of the open cunt beneath it. Mrs. Johanson thrust her pussy up at the man. She grabbed his cock and guided it into her cunt. Hawthorne needed no further invitation. He pushed his cock into the woman's slippery fuckhole and swiftly fucked it into the hilt. As he fucked his cock in, the woman wrapped her legs tightly around his waist and pulled him against her.

Jennifer watched in awe as the two went at it like wild animals. She stared hard at the man's pistoning cock. His prick slipped and slid easily as they fucked each other hard. Each time his big cock pulled back, Jennifer could see the thick, slippery cunt cream that coated it. The woman's cuntlips bulged outward on each outstroke. When his cock flicked back in, the woman's cuntlips folded back in and expanded widely as they were split by his thick cock root. Jennifer could see the man's big balls slapping against the lady's ass with each deep stroke. From the way they were swinging and slapping against the woman's soft asscheeks, Jennifer wondered how the man kept from hurting himself as he fucked.

Mrs. Johanson was going crazy with lust. Her eyes were closed, and her mouth was open. She constantly moaned her excitement, thrusting her cunt hard against the man's fucking cock. Her hips ground from side to side each time his cock hit bottom as she enjoyed herself to the fullest. She held onto Hawthorne with her arms and legs wrapped tightly around his lean body. Every now and then, Jennifer could see a small squirt of pussy juice shooting out of the woman's cunt as the man pulled his cock back. There was no mistaking the fact that the lady was having the time of her life.

Hawthorne, too, was clearly having a good time. He grunted and groaned, powerfully hammering his cock in and out. His eyes were closed as he panted his lust. He war fucking the woman like a madman. He would pull his cock back until his bulbous prickhead came in to view. Then, he would push hard against the lady's gratefully yielding body and drive his cock as deeply into her fuckhole as it would go. He ground hard against the woman, making his cock dig in, the thick root forcing her cuntlips wide open. Holding the woman tightly, he rode high in the saddle so his cock stroked her clit as they fucked. Thrusting as deeply as possible, he rode her hard and fast. Loving it, the woman met his every thrust with her clutching pussy.

Soon Mary's body began stiffening as she felt herself about to cum. Moaning loudly, she gripped the man harder and fucked him faster. The waves of pleasure raced from her cunt and clit to her brain.

"Larry! Ohhh, I'm-I'm gonna cum!" Bucking furiously, she came. Jennifer watched in awe.

Mary panted in quick, sharp gasps. Her face turned beet red as her muscles convulsed. Her cunt squeezed and clamped down, grabbing at the man's cock. Her legs wildly jerked. She kicked the man with her heels, trying to cram him into her cunt, balls and all. Delighted squeals escaped between her moans until with a final heave, her body relaxed into a more gentle fucking motion.

Even as the woman's climax was ending, Larry's was just about to begin. The lady's juicy cunt wrung his cock in its tight, wet grip. His cock swelled to the bursting point. His balls tightened up. He fucked harder. His mind grew numb. His cock spasmed. Howling his desire, he came.

"Ohhh, you cunt! I'm cumming! Uuuhhh!" he groaned.

Fucking into the woman's cunt, his cock blew out a spray of cum. His cock throbbed mightily, deeply inside the lady's open pussy. Convulsions wracked his body. He moaned incoherently as his muscles tensed and spasmed. As his cock pumped, gobs of his cum clung to the sides of it and dripped between Mary's spread thighs. Several thrusts later, he slumped onto her body and relaxed, completely worn out. After clinging to each other for several minutes, they rolled apart and lay on their backs on the floor. Gradually, their gazes focused on the young girl.

Mary said, "You know what to do, Jennifer. Clean his cock."

Jennifer looked at the man's cock. It was reddened from its recent use. Big gobs of cum stuck to its sides, to his balls, and to the hair surrounding his cock. His whole prick was coated with sticky wetness. Shakily, Jennifer crawled between his legs, growing more excited as she thought of licking up the cum.

The strong aroma of cock cream and cunt juices filled the girl's nostrils as her face lowered. She inhaled deeply. Her cunt was dripping more cream, aching to be touched and fondled. The smell only served to make her even hornier. Seeing a glob of cum on the man's inner thigh, she bent to lick it up.

Her tongue snaked out, scooping up the cum. Jennifer held still for just a moment, savoring the flavor of the sticky stuff. The cum worked its magic on her brain, and she quickly bent back down to her task. Reaching up and running her hands over the man's flat belly, she opened her mouth and started licking with gusto. Her tongue slid along Hawthorne's inner thighs. It went underneath his balls to his asshole, then back up to his balls. With her nose right next to the man's c k and balls, Jennifer kept inhaling deeply as she eagerly licked up the spilt juices.

She licked her way around the man's balls, then began licking back and forth over them. After carefully licking them clean, she worked her way to the root of his cock. She licked wildly as the aroma drove her insane with lust. Her tongue couldn't stop moving. It was simply too good to resist.

Hungrily, she kissed and licked the smooth underside of the man's prick. Her hands roved down and she started massaging the area around his cock and balls. She licked up the length of his cock until she got to his prickhead, and then she licked back down. Her lips swiftly opened and closed on his sensitive cockflesh, like those of a fish out of water. All the while, her tongue was tracing gentle circles as she swabbed up the slippery juices.

She moved her mouth around to the side of the man's cock. Pushing against his prick to lick up the cream, she nudged it over to the other side. With her mouth open, she pursued it. Her mouth fastened to the side of it. She lightly sucked while rapidly flicking her tongue over his wet prick skin. She slid her mouth over and around his cockflesh to the other side. Working her head up and down, she vacuumed up all the cum on his cockshaft. Now all that was left was matted in the man's cock hairs and on his cockhead.

Temporarily ignoring his cock-knob, which was still seeping cum, Jennifer slid her tongue back down to the root. Burying her face in the man's hairs, she wet them thoroughly with her tongue. By the time she was through, the cum which had been matted in the hairs was nowhere to be seen. It had gone on its way don the girl's throat.

Grabbing ahold of the man's cock root, Jennifer held it upright. Gazing dreamily at the cum splattered on his prickhead, her face mov-ed closer. Her lips parted, and with one gulp, she wrapped her lips around his reddened cock crown. Nodding her head as she slid her lips around his big prick-knob, she flicked her tongue over his piss-slit at the same time. Gratefully, she savored the taste of cum. Sucking and licking, she began pumping with her hand. Though his cock had been almost limp, his prickshaft now grew a little until it stood at half mast. The girl licked and sucked, but could not get it any stiffer.

Squirming under her tongue, Hawthorne said, "That's enough, baby. Now, clean Mary, too." He nodded toward Mrs. Johanson, who lay back with her legs still spread wide apart.

Jennifer looked between the woman's legs and saw her gaping fuckhole. Thick, white cream was smeared all over between her legs. It dripped from her cunt, which glistened from her cunt hairs to her asshole. Breathing faster, Jennifer crawled between the woman's legs and started to clean the area around her pussy with her tongue.

She dove in and licked the wet juices off the woman's inner thighs. In response, the lady's body jerked at the soft touch of the girl's tongue. Jennifer licked around the woman's swollen cuntlips and up to her matted pussy hair. Her mouth paused at each of the scattered globs of cum. They swiftly disappeared into her mouth. When all the wads had been eaten, the girl ran her tongue all over the woman's cunt hairs to clean them completely. Finished, she slid her tongue to the lady's cuntslit.

She licked up and down Mary's cuntlips, and then started working her tongue in between them. The shockingly delicious taste of cum filled her mouth. As her tongue touched Mary's smooth inner cuntflesh, Jennifer flicked her tongue faster and faster. Like a wild woman, she licked up and down Mary's open cuntslit. Pushing her tongue deeper in between the swollen folds of pussy flesh, she spread the lady's cuntlips apart to get in. Her tongue swirled into Mary's fuckhole, loving the just-fucked flavor of her warm pussy.

Extending her tongue as far as possible, Jennifer moved her head from side to side. Her tongue performed in strong, rapid circles. She licked the woman's cunt to get all the cum she could. Pulling up, she licked up to the lady's clit. Circling Mary's fucknub with her lips, she exerted a gentle sucking while flicking it with her tongues It didn't take long before Johanson was squealing with delight.

The woman raised her legs and she locked them around Jennifer's neck. Her body was tensing as she readied herself for another climax. She put her hands on each side of the young girl's face as Jennifer's tongue diddled her clit and cunt. Panting hard, she babbled and moaned as she was driven out of her mind by her lust.

Jennifer kept licking and sucking. Moaning softly with her eyes closed, she felt hands touching her cunt. Without slowing her tongue, she spread her legs apart. A hand was massaging her inner thighs and the area around her cunt. Then fingers separated her cuntlips and started rubbing up and down her pussyslit. Without knowing what she was doing, Jennifer started gyrating her pussy in pleasure. Still, her lips and tongue worked on Mary's clit.

Feeling fingers pushing into her cunt, Jennifer pushed two of her own fingers into Johanson's pussy. As the fingers started sawing in and out of her pussy, Jennifer's fingers sawed in and out of the lady's cunt. Fingers rubbed over her clit. Jennifer's tongue flicked faster and more eagerly over Mary's clit.

Jennifer knew Mary was feeling good when she

felt the woman's legs tighten around her neck. The grip on her head also tightened as the woman screamed, "Ohhhhh, ohhhhh, aaaaaahbhhhhhhh! I'm g-gonna cum, you sweet little bitch! Suck my cunt!"

Jennifer's fingers pistoned faster and harder. She sucked and licked furiously. The woman's cunt slammed onto her face and ground hard against her mouth. She felt Mary's whole body tensing and convulsing in climax. Her head bobbed up and down with the lady's spasms. She tried to keep her mouth glued to Johanson's clit as the woman frenziedly bucked in pleasure. She could feel the woman's cunt squeezing and clamping down around her fucking fingers. Incoherent moans shot from the woman's throat as she slammed herself hard against the young girl's soft mouth.

Jennifer's own pussy seemed to expand. The fingers inside it worked furiously in and out. They swirled around in circles, rubbing all of the soft flesh inside her tender pussy. The fingers tending her clit rubbed around it, then closed and pinched and pulled. When she felt the man's whole palm massaging her clit, the breath shot out of her lungs as she came.

Even as she felt the woman's body relaxing under her touch, her own body convulsed in supreme pleasure. Her muscles straining hard, she spasmed again and again. Without realizing what she was doing, she grabbed the woman's legs and held onto her for dear life. The spasms wracked her body from head to foot. Her cunt snapped at the sliding fingers. Cunt cream gushed from her fuckhole, and the two fingers slipped and slid with greater case than before. Her ass jerked crazily from side to side as she moaned.

"Mmnnnn, yeahhhh, aaahhhh, oh, oh, oh!" she cried.

Her body spasmed repeatedly, until, finally, she relaxed. She rested her head on the woman's cunt mound, exhausted. Slowly, her brain cleared. Still numbed, she felt the fingers pulling out of her fuckhole. As her cunt emptied, she felt her own pussy juices dripping down her thighs. Dizzy, she rolled onto her back.

"Lift your legs and spread 'em," said Hawthorne. As the girl did as she was told, Hawthorne got between them and started wiping up her cunt cream with his fingers. His cock was still frozen at half mast, and could be raised no farther.

Jennifer smiled as she felt the man's fingers tickling her thighs and cunt. She opened her eyes as the tickling stopped. The man held his fingers near the girl's face. The smell of her cunt drifted into her nose.

"Lick my fingers."

Jennifer didn't even have to think twice about it. She held his hand steady. Her tongue snaked out of her mouth. Tasting the juices of her own cunt excited her. Lapping until the man's fingers were clean, she pulled them into her mouth and sucked. Satisfied at last, she pulled them back out of her mouth. Now she wished she had done as her boyfriend had suggested and licked up her own cunt cream long ago.

The man and the woman looked at the girl's smooth, taut body. Though they had had enough for the moment, they knew it would not be long before they wanted more. The girl was hot. She was what they had long been looking for.

Mrs. Johanson said, "Okay, Jennifer. You can go now. I'll be calling you back to see me soon. And when I do, I expect you to come quickly and do exactly as I say. Don't forget that."

"Yeah, and that goes for me, too, Jennifer," added Hawthorne.

"All right," she answered. "I-I'll do anything you say." Her body trembling, she got dressed. The others did the same.

Jennifer went to the door and she turned to look at them. Her voice caught in her throat, but she forced the words out.

"Please-make it soon."

CHAPTER 6

Jennifer was sitting in her morning class when she received the summons. Her teacher came over to her and told her she was wanted in the vice-principal's office.

With a rush of excitement, she entered the office area. Her pussy was already moistening As Hawthorne met her at the door to his office.

Jennifer looked around, saying, "Wh-where's Mrs. Johanson?"

"She couldn't make it today. Fuck 'er. There's somebody waiting in my office who wants to meet you. Remember, baby. You're to do exactly as you're told at all times. Now, let's go in."

Jennifer went in and saw the football coach sitting in a chair in front of the vice-principal's desk. Coach Dave O'Reilly sat there grinning at her with a lustful leer. He was short, stocky and muscular. His brown hair was short. His brown eyes gleamed out at her, making her knees tremble as her heart melted.

"Hello, Jennifer," he said. "It's time we got acquainted."

Goosebumps broke out on her skin. "G-good morning, coach," She looked down at the floor.

Hawthorne went around his desk and he sat down. "Stand in front of my desk, Jennifer. There, beside the coach's chair."

Jennifer did as instructed, wondering what they had planned. She didn't have long to wait to find out. She stood next to O'Reilly's chair and slightly in front of him, with her ass toward him. Shivers rushed up and down her body as she felt the man's hand rubbing her leg. Almost immediately, her cunt started swelling.

She tried to stand still as the coach's hand slid over and around her legs, one at a time. His hand slid under her dress and in between her thighs to caress the sensitive flesh just beneath her cunt. Before she could stop herself, she opened her legs and moaned. Hawthorne sat behind his desk, watching with a smile on his face.

Coach O'Reilly said, "That's it, baby. Damn, your skin is so soft and smooth. I can feel the heat coming through your panties, too." His leer grew broader. Jennifer blushed.

The man's hand rose higher and lightly tickled her cunt through her panties. It slid back between her legs to her ass. Jennifer felt her ass being rubbed, fondled and massaged as the coach pinched and pulled her asscheeks. After several moments of this exquisite treatment, the girl felt the map's hand gliding back to her cunt. He rubbed over her pussylips and up to her clit. Gently massaging through her panties, his hand pressed on her clit and stroked the whole sensitive area. Before Jennifer knew what she was doing, she had thrust her cunt onto the man's hand. Another moan shot from her throat. Growing ashamed of herself, she tried to stay in control of her body's desires. She forced herself to remain still. It was hard to do with the coach rubbing her clit. Before many more seconds had passed, the girl was again gyrating her cunt in response to the extreme pleasure.

Coach O'Reilly chuckled, "Hot little bitch, aren't you. Well, we're gonna take care of that, baby. Let's see what you look like with your clothes off. I wanna see your pussy."

Jennifer looked at Hawthorne, who nodded and said, "Go on. Do as he says."

Jennifer took off her dress and she cast it aside. The coach stared hard at her firm young body, clad only in bra and bikini panties. The men watched while Jennifer unhooked her bra and slowly slid out of it. As her full tits came into view, they stared even harder. The girl's tits were fine and firm. It was plain that the girl was aroused, from the way her nipples stood out and puckered up.

The girl stood before them, wallowing in their attention. Her body was flushed with excitement as she hooked her fingers in her panties, then pulled them down. Her tender pussy with its sparse cover of light-brown hair was now exposed. A hard lump was growing in the coach's pants as he stared at the young girl's smooth flesh. Reaching out, he pulled the girl to him.

Jennifer arched her back and moaned as the man pressed his mouth onto her belly. The man's arms went around her waist as he kissed her body. He cupped her asscheeks while he kissed her warm belly, then began sliding his mouth higher. Jennifer bent down to put her tits in front of the man's face. The coach kissed and licked his way all around Jennifer's tits. Then he began licking in an inward spiral to her nipples, one at a time. Jennifer couldn't help but groan her delight at the sensation. She felt her nipple being sucked and licked, then a finger slid between her thighs.

Her clit was throbbing as the coach rubbed the full length of his finger along her cuntslit. It was feeling damn good when the coach pulled 'the girl's mouth down to his. Their tongues met and entwined with each other. They licked over each other's mouth and lips, and then their tongues began darting from mouth to mouth. Jennifer opened her mouth and pulled back her tongue. The coach pushed his own tongue into the girl's mouth, swirling it around and over her tongue. When his tongue pulled

back, Jennifer swiftly pushed her tongue into the man's mouth. Her cunt tingled under the soft caress of the man's finger. She wanted to be fucked.

"Ohhh, fuck me, please! I want it!"

The coach pulled back and laughed, "Not yet, honey. Be quiet now. We'll tell you what to do, and when. You'll be taken care of." He bent and kissed her belly, then moved lower. Falling to his knees in front of the girl, O'Reilly started eating her pussy.

Jennifer was quivering with desire. The coach wrapped his arms around her ass. The feel of his tongue sliding down her belly to her cunt was driving her wild. The coach's mouth tickled her cunt hairs before moving farther down. To her disappointment, the wonderful tongue slid around her clit instead of over it. To her delight, it started slithering over her tender cuntlips. The man licked up and down the girl's cuntlips, pausing every now and then to lick the sensitive area at her inner thighs. When she felt the man's tongue licking toward the center of her cunt, Jennifer gave an appreciative sigh.

Coach O'Reilly was going crazy between the young girl's legs. After swabbing her downy pussylips, he carefully spread her pussy open and looked inside. He stared hard at the moist, pink cuntflesh, and his cock throbbed in his pants. He dove in with his tongue. His tongue stabbed deep into the girl's warm fuckhole. It wiggled back and forth, and from side to side, before slipping out, then plunging back in again. Inhaling deeply, he hungrily ate her out while holding her pussylips spread open.

Jennifer spread her legs wider, tossing her head in pleasure. She smiled as she felt the man's hot breath and warm tongue on her pussy. Her clit was swollen and pulsing in lust. Thrusting her cunt onto the man's face, she wanted him to lick and suck her clit for a while. Still, it felt damn good to have his tongue deep inside her cunt. As if in answer to her prayers, she soon felt O'Reilly's tongue sliding out of her fuckhole and up her cunt slit.

The coach was sucking and licking the young girl's pussy like a starving man. The girl's smooth, wet cuntflesh against his tongue was very tasty. He slid the full length of his tongue along the girl's cuntslit. After rubbing it up and down, he licked up to her clit. His tongue swirled around and around her swollen fuck nub. Then he flicked his tongue directly over it several times. He slipped his tongue along the girl's cunt slit, with the base of his tongue on her clit, and licked up. His tongue dragged across Jennifer's clit, making her squeal with pleasure. By the time be was through lick-ing her cunt and fastened his lips around her clit, the girl was undulating her hips and thrusting her pussy onto the man's face. He sucked gently on her clit, and pushed a finger into her fuckhole.

Jennifer gasped, "Ohhhhh, uhhhh, good."

Her breathing was coming faster now, and her skin was flushing with excitement. As much as she tried to control herself, she couldn't help grinding her pussy from side to side. The finger sawed in and out of her cunt. The pleasure was getting better and better for the girl, when the man stood up and yanked down his pants.

The coach sat in the chair and stroked his seven-inch cock. Staring hard at the girl's taut body, he said, "Get on your knees, honey. Suck me off. I wanna cum in your mouth."

Jennifer, her cunt burning, stared at his thick cock. Her clit was throbbing. She craved release. She desperately wanted to cum. Looking at the two men, she knew that they wouldn't let her cum until they were ready. She was so horny that she would do anything. Mewling her desire, she dropped to her knees.

Jennifer grabbed his cock as he let go of it. Her hand could barely fit around his prickshaft. She started licking his balls, gently jerking him off. She licked his ball-sac until it glistened. She moved her hand out of the way so her tongue could get at his cock. Feverishly, she licked up and down the underside of the cockshaft. Turning his prick from side to side, she licked each side of it, and then the top. After his whole cockshaft shined, she moved to his prick head.

"Ohhhh, yeah, that's it, Jennifer. I like a lot of tongue," he groaned. Holding the back of her head, he spread his legs wider.

Jennifer licked over his piss hole, sucking up the sticky fluid seeping from within. Smacking her lips, she started licking around his piss hole in ever-widening circles. She pulled the man's cock this way and that while she licked. Hearing his happy sighs made her face glow with pleasure. She was now ready to suck him.

Opening her mouth, she slid her slick lips over the coach's prickhead. Pausing with her lips locked around his cock crown, she flicked her tongue over and around it. She started bobbing her head up and down while stroking his prick with her hand. Each time her head bobbed down, her mouth sucked in more cock. All the while, she gently squeezed his fucker in her lips and bathed it with her tongue. The coach egged her on with his hands, guiding her face up and down and from side to side as she sucked.

When she had taken all she could take into her mouth, she started a slow pumping. She easily slid her lips back up to his cockhead, dragging her tongue along the underside as she did so. Then she reversed direction and drove her head back down. As she got the hang of it, she tickled his balls and massaged the base of his cock with the other hand.

Watching the stimulating scene made the vice-principal extremely horny. He got up to get a better view of the young girl's wet mouth sliding up and down the coach's cock. With his cock almost ready to burst out of his pants, he pulled them down, then started jacking off. Soon he could take it no more and got down behind Jennifer. He started playing with her pussy and ass.

Jennifer felt the man's hands between her legs, and she was grateful. The fingers cupped her pussy and massaged the whole mound of her cunt. Then they slid over her asscheeks. It felt good as her ass was massaged from top to bottom, then from side to side. Her body filled with feelings of pleasure as fingers slid down her asscrack. They circled her asshole several times before tickling her puckered anus mouth. She moaned around the big cock in her mouth as her asshole throbbed with pleasure. Reflexively, she began twitching the tight muscle. She wanted something more, but didn't quite realize what. The fingers slid to her cunt.

Hawthorne knew Jennifer liked having her asshole played with when the ring of muscle puckered up under his touch. Making a mental note to make a speedy return to her asshole, he slid his fingers to her cunt, and then into it.

Jennifer thrilled to feel two fingers plunging in and out of her pussy. After several deep strokes, they pulled out and started circling her asshole. They circled, pressing more firmly than before. Jennifer arched her back in pleasure, thrusting her ass out and up. Chills rushed up and down her spine at the strange, but good sensation. As the fingers pushed harder, she could feel her asshole opening up.

The fingers pulled away, and one drove deeply into her pussy. It wiggled back and forth, picking up plenty of her cream, then pulled out. It pushed against her asshole and started working inside. Jennifer trembled, moaning. It felt so good that she wondered why she hadn't pushed a finger up her ass before. When O'Reilly squeezed her head and pumped it up and down, the girl started sucking again. Feeling his hot cock along her tongue only increased the pleasure she got from having her asshole fingered. She pushed back against the pleasure-giving finger. She wanted it all.

Hawthorne smiled at the girl's horniness. Goddamn, she was a hot little bitch. He pushed his finger all the way up her ass. He started sliding it in and out, while the girl responded with muffled groans. He felt the girl's asshole squeezing tightly around his finger, and his cock strained even harder. Her shithole was so fucking tight. The more he finger-fucked her asshole, and the more Jennifer thrust her ass back at him, the more he realized that he wanted to put his cock in there. He wanted to fuck the young girl's tight asshole.

Jennifer tried to concentrate on sucking the coach's cock. With the good feelings radiating from her asshole, however, it was difficult. She licked and sucked, massaging his cock and balls at the same time. The finger sliding deeply into her ass was sending her to heights of pleasure she had never thought possible. She clamped her asshole around it and ground her ass from side to side.

Hawthorne pulled his finger out of the girl's ass. He rubbed her asscheeks, then spread them apart. After staring hungrily at her puckered brown shithole, he bent his face to it. He inhaled deeply, and then lashed out with his tongue. He licked around her asshole, then over the ridge. After flicking his tongue over her anus several times, he started pushing into it with his tongue. To spread her ass even more, he moved his thumbs closer to Jennifer's asshole. With his thumbs helping to open her brown shithole, he penetrated it with his tongue.

Jennifer mewled in delight as the man's velvety a tongue darted into her asshole. She loved it as her ass was spread open and his tongue stabbed into her slitter. As fingers rubbed her clit and played with her cunt at the same time, it felt even better. She sucked madly on the cock in her mouth, getting hotter all the time. She felt her cunt expanding even more, and this time she knew she was going to cum. Even as she thought it, she was disappointed. The tongue and fingers were withdrawn.

Startled, she lifted her head. Turning, she saw Hawthorne racing around his desk and reaching into a drawer. Before she could see anything else, her head was roughly pulled back down. She sucked.

Hawthorne grabbed at the tube of jelly in his desk. He hurried to get back behind the girl. He squeezed a generous amount of the lube on his fingers, then started lubing her asshole. His cock throbbed as he pushed first one, and then two greased fingers into her anus to get it ready for fucking.

Jennifer sucked harder when she felt his fingers again driving into her ass. When the one pulled out and was quickly replaced with two, her asshole stretched at the intrusion. She gasped as her slitter expanded. The fingers dug into her trembling asshole, and she moan-ed in pleasure as they went deep. It was like nothing she had ever felt before. Her mouth worked harder as the fingers plunged in and out, coating the inside of her asshole with grease.

Working her ass from side to side, she madly licked and sucked O'Reilly's cock. Every few moments, she would stop, pull up her head, and run her tongue all over his prick. She would lick and kiss his cockhead, then slide her lips and tongue underneath. Her tongue would glide over the sides and along the top of his prickshaft. Then she would open her mouth and gobble up his stiff cock once again. She could feel the man's body stiffening as his cock swelled in her mouth.

Groaning in ecstasy, Dave pumped the girl's head up and down his swollen cock. "Ohhhh, baby. I'm gonna cum! Keep sucking! D-don't stop! Ohhhh, suck it!" His grip tightened and his fingers twisted the girl's hair. He thrust his cock hard into her mouth, and his cock exploded in a flood of hot cum.

Jennifer gobbled and sucked. Her head rocked up and down as she tried to keep his big cock from choking her. She felt his prick expanding. Spasms ran its length, and then the cum spurted into her mouth. Great jets of thick, warm cum sprayed over her tongue and hit the back of her mouth. She sucked hard. The man's cock throbbed in powerful spasms. The foaming cum filled her mouth with its fine flavor. She kept her lips tightly locked to milk the man's cock dry. Even as the man's spasms came slower and further apart, the girl kept sucking strongly. She savored the heady, exotic taste of cum, rolling her tongue all around his pisshole and cockhead. As the man slumped back in his scat, Jennifer sucked more gently. Wanting to extract all the cum she could get, she softly nursed on it like a newborn babe. Finally, sensing she had gotten it all, she started pulling up, careful not to let a drop of cock cream slip out of her mouth. Before her head was all the way up, the coach stopped her.

"Hold it, Jennifer. Hold my cock in your mouth until I tell you to take it out," he said. He pulled her head back down.

Jennifer rested her face in the man's lap, her mouth full of cock and cum. She was content. She lay there, dreaming of how good it was, with her mouth full and her asshole plugged with two fingers.

Larry slowly worked his fingers in and out of the girl's ass. Driving his fingers deep, he played with her pussy with his other hand. He rubbed a finger up and down her swollen cunt slit, then pushed it inside her fuckhole. When the girl pushed back at him and squeezed her cunt and asshole around his fingers, his cock twitched. He sawed both pairs of fingers in and out, grinding them from side to side at the same time. Then he pulled the fingers out of her cunt, sliding them up to her clit. There, he started massaging the swollen little fuck nub.

Jennifer relaxed completely and enjoyed it. Still holding O'Reilly's cock in her mouth, she felt her cunt throbbing. When the fingers started frigging her clit, she knew without a shadow of a doubt that this time she was going to cum.

Her pussy throbbed in delight. Her mind fogged over until she thought she would scream with pleasure. The goodness welled up inside her as her muscles tensed. When she thought she could take it no more, she was hit by spasms of climax. Her body trembled as she came. Her cunt and asshole simultaneously clenched and unclenched. Her breath came in a rush as she shook from head to foot. She spasmed until she lay exhausted, her body wracked with sobs of pleasure.

When it was over, Hawthorne told her, "Spread your asscheeks. I'm gonna fuck you in the ass."

CHAPTER 7

Jennifer's first thought was of the pain. His cock was so big. But then, still in the dream world of her climax, she started liking the idea. She worked her asshole around the man's two fingers, which were still deeply embedded in the brown shit hole between her asscheeks. Yeah, it was something new to try. Her body aflame with desire, she grabbed her asscheeks and spread them apart.

"All right! Fuck me there!"

Quickly, Hawthorne pulled out his fingers and greased his cock. When he was done, he moved between her asscheeks and pushed his cockhead against the girl's asshole. Holding his cock in place, he gave it a gentle nudge. The girl's tight asshole hardly opened. Feeling the tightness of Jennifer's asshole, he groaned. His cock was throbbing in anticipation of fucking all the way to the balls into the young girl's asshole.

Jennifer spread her firm asscheeks wider as the hot hardness of the man's cock pushed between them. The growing pressure made her asshole stretch, and a stab of pain shot through her body. Her tender brown asshole expanded until she grunted. Hawthorne graciously halted the advance of his giant cock.

He stared between the girl's spread asscheeks. Seeing how her little asshole was stretched over half his cockhead, he was filled with the desire to fuck his cock deep. Holding himself back, he said, "Relax, Jennifer. It might hurt a little at first, but if you relax, it'll get better fast. If it hurts too much, tell me and I'll take it out." He grinned behind the girl's back as he told the lie. The coach grinned back at him. They both knew that once his cock was in, it wasn't going back out before leaving a load of cum deep inside the girl's ass.

Jennifer moaned. It was feeling better. She rested her mouth around O'Reilly's cock root as she relaxed her asshole. Yeah, it was feeling much better. With her asshole slightly punctured by the man's prickhead, she felt an itch deep inside her shit hole that ached to be scratched. The only way to satisfy it was for the man to fuck her asshole deep. She spread her asscheeks wider and pushed back against the man's cock.

Hawthorne worked his cockhead back and forth an inch at a time, careful not to let it slip all the way out. With each pump, the girl's asshole was forced to open a little more, his cock pushed a little deeper.

Jennifer kept her asscheeks pulled wide apart and pushed back. She could feel her tight shithole expanding more than ever before. Her ass stretched until she almost thought it would tear. She fought to relax her asshole to let it open, and then his big cock knob popped past the restraining muscle. Uncontrollably, her asshole clamped shut behind the man's cockhead, holding it tightly and comfortably, inside. Hawthorne moaned as Jennifer put the squeeze on him.

"Goddamn, that's tight. Uuuuuhhhh," he sighed.

Jennifer's muscles were taut with the strain. Waves of pain radiated from her asshole. Her toes were curled up and her face was flushed. She fought to relax as his monstrous cock knob started easing back and forth. The gentle stroking inside her ass soothed her anus, sending signals of a goodness she had never known racing to her brain. The strange feeling as his cockhead stretched her asshole deeper swiftly began overriding the pain. She felt every little bit of forward motion his cock made, and was enjoying it more with each thrust. Her asshole opened up more fully, and the man's rock-hard cock fucked deeper. She panted in joy.

"Ohhh, Mr. Hawthorne, oh, yes!"

Hawthorne was pleased with himself. He had known that once his big prick knob got into her asshole, it would soon feel good to the girl. Now he stared between Jennifer's firm ass-cheeks. Half his cock was buried in her stretched anus. Goddamn, it was so fucking exciting to watch a girl's tender asshole stretching wide open to take his cock.

Holding onto Jennifer's waist, he moved his hips from side to side to open her asshole a little more. Pausing in his fucking, he ran his hands along Jennifer's smooth hips and waist, and he cupped her tits. He rubbed his hands over them, squeezing her nipples. Massaging her tits in gentle circles, he started stroking her asshole with his cock once again. He knew she liked it when she started moving with him.

Jennifer dreamily closed her eyes. She shivered, feeling the hands playing with her tits and nipples. When she felt his cock again moving in her asshole, she couldn't help moving her ass, too. The pleasure doubled. She pulled her asscheeks as wide as they would go and pushed against the man's cock. It slid deeper, and her asshole started swelling even more to take his thick prick root. She humped her ass back and forth, squeezing his cock in her asshole as she fucked him right back. She pushed against him, while relaxing her powerful anus. His cock fucked in, stretching her little asshole wider. Then she clamped Hawthorne's stiff cock in a vise-like grip. She ground her ass in circles, then pulled away. As her tight asshole slid along the man's cock, his slippery cockflesh was satisfyingly pulled.

"That's it, baby. Milk my cock with your ass. Work your asshole, Jennifer, ohhhhhhhhh, yeahhhhhh!" He moved his hands back down and wrapped them around her waist. No longer able to hold back, he pushed the remaining bit of cock into her ass with a powerful thrust.

A grunt burst from Jennifer's throat. Extreme pleasure rippled out from her stuffed asshole. The waves rolled over her cunt and were amplified. Together, her pussy and asshole tingled with lust. The pulses of goodness rushed throughout her body from head to toe. She pushed hard against Hawthorne's belly, clenching her tender brown anus as tightly as she could. Unconsciously, her tongue rolled around the coach's cock, still held snugly between her lips. Her asshole quivered in delight.

Moaning, Hawthorne ground hard against the young girl's soft asscheeks. He worked his cock from side to side, then started fucking. Gently at first, he pulled his cock back until his prickhead almost came out. Then he firmly slid his prick deeply into her slippery brown asshole all the way to his balls. When his cock hit bottom, he ground hard between Jennifer's asscheeks. It gratified him to see and feel the girl fucking him right back. One of his hands slipped down between her thighs to caress her pussy.

Jennifer worked her ass, moaning softly over Coach O'Reilly's balls. She trembled as Hawthorne's hand tickled her pussy. The length of his finger lay along her cuntslit and started massaging it from her clit to her asshole. Electric thrills raced to her brain. The pleasure she got from her fucked asshole multiplied the signals shooting from her pussy. Even as she was filled with the fever of her lust, she could feel the coach's cock once again swelling inside her mouth.

The coach had been quietly sitting back, watching Hawthorne ass-fuck the girl. In the hazy aftermath of his orgasm, he had been content to rest while the girl mouthed his cock. But now the scene was getting to him. He saw how much Jennifer was enjoying herself as she got Hawthorne's cock up her ass. He thought how tight and warm her asshole must be. He visualized himself fucking the young girl's asshole, and his cock started reviving in her mouth. He vowed that soon he would take his turn fucking her in the ass. For now, though, he would satisfy himself in her mouth.

Hawthorne's fingers slipped up and down the girl's soft pussy. He worked his cock from side to side in her ass. He paid careful attention to her clit, knowing how much it would increase the pleasure of getting ass-fucked. Massaging the entire area around the girl's clit, he humped steadily against her soft, smooth asscheeks. Each time he pulled his cock back for the next thrust, the girl's powerful brown anus squeezed his prick in a tight, slippery grip. When he fucked back deeply into her asshole, the girl relaxed and pushed back at him. The man could not help groaning in pleasure at the clutching, milking warmth of the young girl's ass.

Jennifer's mind was being taken over by thoughts of Hawthorne's ass-fucking cock. She quivered to feel her asshole stretching open each time his prick fucked in to the balls. She felt her anus walls contracting as his cock pulled back and she clenched the muscle tightly. Every time the man pulled back, the girl felt like her ass was being emptied. Every time the man fucked deep, she experienced an ecstatic fullness that could only come from having a thick, hard cock plunging deeply into her asshole and stretching it wide open. Her clit throbbed in swollen excitement. She could feel her pussy creaming. As her clit pulsed under the man's fingers, Jennifer knew she was going to cum.

She ground her ass from side to side as the explosion seemed near at hand. She could feel Hawthorne's fingers thoroughly working over and around her clit. They massaged faster and more firmly. At the same time, the man behind her fucked her more furiously. Together, they bucked and groaned in enjoyment. Jennifer's heated body tensed and convulsed as she came.

The breath shot out of her lungs. Her asshole twitched and spasmed. The juices gushed from her cunt. Her mouth gripped O'Reilly's cock, and she sucked it in a strong vacuum. Her eyes were tightly closed. Her hands gripped her asscheeks in an unconscious death grip as she tried to tear them off her body. Her toes were curled up, and her legs were spread wide. Not knowing where she was or what was going on around her, she joyously drove her quivering asshole against the man's balls and ground back hard.

Hawthorne, his head thrown back, was enjoying the full benefits of Jennifer's fluttering asshole as the girl spasmed in climax. Held in the grip of her brown shithole, Hawthorne's cock swelled in fuck-lust. The girl's asshole rapidly pinched the man's cock all along its length as her body was wracked with convulsions. The vice-principal slammed into her, fucking his cock as deeply as it would go and pulling the girl against him as he ground hard. His grunts came more frequently as his prick was milked so well. When he sensed that the girl's climax, had ended, he slowed down. Concentrating, he tried to keep himself from shooting his load too soon. The pleasure was so great that he wanted it to last as long as possible. However, no matter how long it lasted, it would not be long enough.

Jennifer rode her orgasm to the end. She relaxed, her body glowing with satisfaction. It felt so good that she hoped it would never end. As her brain partially cleared, she was able to turn her attention once more to the coach's cock in her mouth. Her mouth was happily full of his stiff cock once again.

Though the coach had been enjoying the scene, now that his cock had come back to life in the girl's warm mouth, he wanted to be sucked off. With his hands, he guided Jennifer's head up and down. Each time he pulled her head down, he twisted it from side to side. The girl obligingly licked and sucked in happiness.

Jennifer was amazed that the man's cock had gotten hard again so quickly. Her mouth was full of the taste of prick and cum, and she wanted a fresh load of cum to savor. Working her mouth like a fish out of water, she lipped and tongued the man's prick. When she got to his cockhead, her tongue swirled around and around. Locking her lips around his big prick knob, she slid them in circles while working her tongue. Then she slowly slid her lips back down the stiff length of his cock. Her head bobbed up and down, helped along by the man's helpfully guiding hands. When she had taken all she could take at once, she started a steady, firm sucking. The man's prick throbbed under the soft caress of her velvety lips and tongue. As she sucked, she did not forget to keep Hawthorne's cock clutched in the slippery grip of her asshole. Her head swam with the excitement of it all.

Though Hawthorne tried to hold back, the soft, wet warmth of Jennifer's slippery, quivering asshole was too much for his cock to bear. His balls tightened. His cock swelled and throbbed. Shivers rushed through his frame. He ass-fucked the girl faster and faster, in long, deep strokes. He pulled his cock back slowly, reveling in the feel of the gripping ring of Jennifer's asshole pistoning the length of his cock. When his cockhead was back far enough, he slammed hard into the girl's ass, burying his cock between her asscheeks in swift, stabbing strokes. The girl came alive under him, hunching her ass up and out to willingly meet his every thrust.

"Oh, baby? I-ahhhh----I-I'm gonna cum!" Hawthorne wheezed. "Oh, work that ass, yeahhhh!" Wrapping his arms around Jennifer's tits, he fucked her hard as his brain and balls exploded in climax.

With a long, low groan, the breath was squeezed out of his lungs. His body tensed and convulsed. With his eyes screwed shut, he ass fucked the girl in a frenzy of lust. His toes were curled as he thrust out with his legs, driving his cock with all his might into the girl's slippery, squeezing shit hole. His blood pressure shot up, making him see stars behind his eyelids. His cock pulsed and sprayed the girl's insides with thick, wet cum.

Jennifer realized Hawthorne was going into climax as his cock stiffened even harder inside her asshole. She fucked him back as hard as she could. Grinding her ass in little circles, she puckered up her asshole and milked his cock with it. She felt it throbbing as cum shot into her spread ass. She slid her brown shit hole all the way down, squeezed it tightly, and ground back hard. Keeping her asshole tightly puckered, she slid it up to his cock knob. Quickly, she opened her anus and slammed down again.

Hawthorne mindlessly spurted cum deep into the young girl's asshole. The man was not aware of anything except the wonderful feel of Jennifer's anus as it held his cock in its wonderful, warm grip. Repeatedly, his cock spasmed. Spurt after hot spurt of cream flooded into the girl's ass. With the added lube, his cock slipped and slid even easier than before. The thick jizz started dripping out as the girl's ass was filled. Hawthorne fucked hard and deep, and then his body reined as the last spurt was delivered. His cock twitched in the girl's clutching asshole as he rested against her warm body.

Jennifer kept sucking. She was in heaven, with one stiff cock in her mouth and another up her ass. It didn't matter that the one up her ass was rapidly softening. It still plugged her little asshole, and that was what counted. Feeling the coach's cock swelling harder in her mouth, she turned her full attention to sucking it.

Coach O'Reilly's grip was slowly tightening on the girl's head and hair. As he got ready to cum, he pulled her head more roughly into his lap. By the time his cock started pulsing, he was fucking Jennifer's mouth in long strokes. He was careful not to shove his cock too far down her throat, but the soft wetness of her eager mouth was about to send him over the brink.

"Oh, suck it, Jennifer! Keep sucking! Ohhh, I'm gonna c-cum in your mouth! Oh, you sweet sucking whore, don't stop! Ahhhh- ahhhhhh-d-don't stop! Aaaarrrrggghhhhh!" His chest heaving, he came hard.

Jennifer gobbled and sucked as the coach's prick erupted in cum. His cock throbbed mightily, and her mouth was flooded with a gush of thick, warm cum. The quick spurts rapidly filled her mouth with the delicious cream. She worked her tongue around his prickhead, washing it in its own cum. She hungrily slurped up the jets of hot cum that filled her mouth. Keeping her lips tightly locked, she didn't let a single drop of the stuff slip out of her mouth. When she felt the coach's body slump back, she kept sucking slowly. As his grip relaxed in her hair, she slid her mouth all the way down and nursed on his cock. Still rolling her tongue around his shrinking prickshaft, she savored to the fullest the great taste of cock and cum.

"A-all right, baby. That's enough," moaned the coach. He let go of the girl's head. She started lifting her mouth.

Jennifer sucked strongly on the way up. Pausing at his cockhead, she licked over his pisshole to get every last drop of cum. Finally, she looked up at him for approval. She saw him leaning back in exhaustion, and was satisfied that she had done a good job. Even as she thought it, she felt Hawthorne's cock slipping out of her ass.

The wonderful fullness was leaving her. Her shit hole was fast emptying of cock. She was filled with disappointment. It had felt so good. As his cockhead hit the inside of her asshole ring, she clenched it shut. His prick knob popped out with a squishing sound. Her asshole shut completely, tingling in satisfaction.

Hawthorne groaned again as the girl clenched her asshole wound his cockhead. His prick flopped out and dangled limply between his legs. It was reddened and completely drained. He looked between Jennifer's asscheeks to burn the vision of her just-fucked asshole into his mind.

With Jennifer on her knees and her ass thrust back, her asscheeks stayed open enough to provide a clear view of her anus. It was reddened and slightly swollen. Grease and cum were smeared around and between her asscheeks. A thin trickle of cum seeped out of her anus, even though it was tightly puckered up. His cock gave a twitch as he thought of how much the girl's asshole had stretched to take it inside. It constantly amazed him to see a little asshole such as Jennifer's opening up fully to take a big cock like his. The soft, warm tightness of a girl's asshole always drove him insane with pleasure. He struggled to his feet.

"Okay, Jennifer. We're through with you for now. You did good today. I hope you liked getting fucked in the ass, 'cause it's gonna be a regular thing from now on." He pulled up his pants as he spoke.

Trembling as she rested on her knees, Jennifer answered, "Yeah, it was good." She smiled a little smile. "I loved it! Thank you. I want you to fuck my ass often, Mr. Hawthorne. Please, tell me you will!"

Chuckling at her eagerness, Hawthorne replied, "Sure I will, honey. From now on, whenever I tell you to, I want you to spread your asscheeks for me. Is that understood?"

"Yes, Sir," she nodded, her asshole fluttering in satisfaction.

Shakily, she got up. She stuffed her bra and panties into her purse and put on her dress without them. Her asshole was still trembling in pleasure. She felt wonderful, alive with a new awareness of the world around her. A smile again flitted across her face, which was glowing with newfound happiness. Getting a tock up the ass was the best thing that had ever happened to her.

As she turned to go, she hesitantly asked, "Will you call me?"

Recognizing her need to be reassured; Hawthorne assured her, "Yeah. You won't have long to wait, Jennifer."

She left, already looking forward to their next meeting.

CHAPTER 8

Jennifer went on to her English class. The taste of cum was in her mouth, and her pussy and asshole throbbed as she sat down. Mr. Brantly, the teacher, was in the process of handing out the final exams. He looked at the girl, noting that she was five minutes late, then returned to the matter at hand.

When he handed Jennifer her paper, he whispered, "Are you ready for the final, Jennifer?"

Jennifer looked into his eyes and experienced a magnetic jolt that ran straight to her cunt, something about him that she had never noticed before. She wondered if her newfound awareness had anything to do with it, then stuttered, "I-I think so, Mr. Brantly." She looked away.

He replied, "Well, I hope so. Good luck." As the man walked away, Jennifer couldn't keep her gaze from straying back to him. She stared at his ass.

Her gaze roved up and down the back of his body. Shaken by sudden desire, she tried to turn her attention to the final. The next hour passed quickly as she wracked her brain. With a deep sense of loss, she realized that the test was too much for her. Still, she kept trying.

Now and then, she glanced up to see Brantly sitting at his desk. The man saw the world through a pair of wire-frame glasses. Light brown hair topped his head. He was of medium build. Each time he caught the girl looking at him, his bright brown eyes would gleam and a smile would flash across his face. Soon, Jennifer was a trembling mass of nerves. She found it impossible to concentrate on the test any further. Her cunt had caused her to fail.

She turned over the test and put her head down in disgust. Thoughts of spurting cock filled her mind. It was not hard for her to imagine herself sucking Brantly's cock. She was surprised to find herself filled with these lustful thoughts about the teacher. She hadn't realized that they were inside her. Then, she guessed the thoughts had been there all along. It was only now that she had recognized them.

Jennifer gave a start as the bell rang, signaling the beginning of her lunch period. Rapidly, the class members turned in their papers and left. By

-the time Jennifer got up, the teacher and herself were the only ones left in the room. Brantly looked at her as he took her paper.

"Looks like you've had a rough time of it."

She tried to smile, but couldn't. "Yeah. It was tough."

"Don't you think you passed it? I know it wasn't that hard."

"Well, Mr. Brantly, to tell you the truth, I think I flunked. I-I just wasn't ready for it," she admitted. As she spoke, she became hypnotized by the man's deep eyes.

"I'm sorry to hear that, Jennifer. Here, we have a little time. It's your lunch break, isn't it?"

"Yes.

"Well, would you like to go over your test with me? You might not have done as badly as you think." He was all sympathy now.

As the girl leaned down, Brantly stared at her ripe tits. Since she wore no bra, her nipples were visible as pinpoints against the front of her dress. He glanced down her body to her feet, then back up again. His cock started growing as he stared at the foxy young girl. He loosened his shirt collar and sat back, trying to remain cool. There was something different about her, he noticed. She wasn't the same girl she had been a few days ago. His heart was pounding as the girl came even closer.

"Oh, could we? You sure you have time?" Jennifer still didn't know what she was going to do. Unconsciously, her breath came quicker as she neared the teacher. Strange, she hadn't noticed before how good looking he was. "That'd be nice.

"Ahem-yeah, I believe we've got time. Let's see. Hmmmmm." He looked at the test and started taking off paints with light pencil marks. With each black mark, Jennifer's fate fell a little further. By the time he was through, it was clear that she had failed miserably.

Brantly sat back. "Jennifer, I'm sorry, but it looks like you did fail. If you'd have told me something, I'd have helped you." He shook his head sadly.

With a sudden burst of inspiration, Jennifer went behind his chair, and leaning over his shoulder, said, "Well. Look at that one. Look at it like this." She reached over the man and pointed, motioning with her hand. By the time she was through explaining her answer, her tits were poking into the man's neck. As she talked into his car, her hot breath burned down the side of his face.

Not sure of what was going on, but hoping it was what he thought it was, Brantly patiently explained why the girl's answer was wrong. His cock continued sprouting inside his pants until it made a huge lump. Jennifer's voice went lower and lower as she talked, and her lips moved closer to the man's face. Now the teacher was sure. Still, he calmly debated with her, waiting for her to make the first move. That would avoid trouble later.

Her heart beating wildly, Jennifer leaned forward to make a point. She knew it was now or never. Her tits pushed against the man's neck. Her hand fell into his lap and squeezed the hard bulge. She breathed into his ear and wetly kissed and licked it. Brantly quickly turned and pulled her face to his. Their mouths fastened together and began hungrily sucking. They slid over each other until Brantly stood up. He pulled the girl to him, pressing his cock against her firm body.

Jennifer turned her face up to Mr. Brantly's, parting her red lips in invitation. Her eyelids were half closed. The man lowered his mouth to hers, and they began a slow exploration of each other's mouth.

Jennifer's tongue snaked out of her mouth and lightly licked over the teacher's lips. It slipped in between them to touch and lick his tongue. Their tongues met and licked and rubbed each other. Both began breathing harder. Their hearts beat faster as they got to know each other better.

They hugged each other tightly and pulled

themselves closer. Their mouths pressed together more firmly. Jennifer felt the teacher's tongue enter her mouth, where it nudged her soft, wet tongue. She began to suck on his tongue until it withdrew. Then she sent her tongue after his until it was all the way in his mouth. She made sure that their tongues did not lose contact. She felt the suction as the man gently sucked her tongue.

Jennifer felt the man's hands roving down her back to her ass. They cupped and fondled each firm ass cheek. Her ass tingled with the sensation as he softly rubbed and fondled the sensitive skin through her skirt. The horny man rubbed her asscheeks in a circular motion, then slid his hands back and forth over them. Jennifer trembled as she felt him grab handfuls of flesh and squeeze her asscheeks. She was going wild as his strong hands alternately grabbed and let go, then grabbed another handful of plump asscheek. Her asshole pulsed with excitement. The hands softly rubbed up and down her back, stopping to grab and fondle her ass, then rubbing back up her back. They lightly slid back down to her ass, and their kissing grew more passionate.

Jennifer moved hex head from side to side, keeping her soft mouth glued to Brantly's. Her mouth wetly slid over his. Her tongue flicked over his lips and nudged his tongue time and time again.

The pleasure mounted, and the passion grew stronger. They moved their mouths in a circular, sliding movement, keeping attached to one another the whole time.

Jennifer rubbed his chest with one hand, rubbing his tits through his shirt. She rubbed first one tit, then the other, massaging his chest with a light touch. Then her hand slowly slid down his chest. It lightly slid down his belly and brushed up against the front of his pants. She detected the huge bulge inside and squeezed.

As they tongued each other, Brantly kept massaging the girl's ass. She, for her part, rubbed the bulge in the front of his pants. She pressed down on his cock, then grabbed its length and squeezed his prickshaft in her hand. She lightly brushed her fingers along its entire length, sending tingles of good feeling running through the teacher's body. His prick twitched and pulsed. Panting in lust for his cock, Jennifer reached for his zipper.

Her hand needed no direction. Jennifer concentrated on kissing and being kissed by the teacher, as her hand unzipped his pants. She reached inside to grab his hard prick, gently easing it out. His cock throbbed in her hand as she stroked and hefted it. She encircled the base with her hand and started stroking the loose skin back and forth in slow motion. She gasped as her A hand measured it. Looking down, she stared at his nine-inch monster prick. Her hand didn't miss a beat, nor did her mouth. Her pussy was hot, and her mouth wanted to be filled with cum.

"Mmmmmmmm, pull your pants down. I wanna suck your cock," she purred.

Without a second's hesitation, the man yanked his pants down to his ankles. His prick bounced up and dawn, stiff and proud. It hung straight out in front of him, at a slight upward angle, throbbing with each beat of his heart.

With a moan of lust, Jennifer dropped to her knees in front of him. She scrutinized his prick, admiring its size and smoothness. She looked at his big balls. They hung loosely down from the base of his prick. Hefting them, she guessed that they probably contained a huge load of cum. She hoped they were ready to spurt into her hot, sucking mouth, because she was going to make them do just that. Her mouth was drawn to his throbbing cockhead.

Jennifer flicked her tongue over the pisshole in his prick tip. She slowly licked back and forth over his cock, probing into it. Then she licked around his cockhead in tiny circles. She grasped the root of his prick with her right hand, slowly jacking it off as she licked it.

Her tongue slid over and over his piss hole. She held his prick and her head still, swirling only her tongue around and around. As Jennifer became more excited, she stiffened her tongue and began shaking her head in circles. She twisted her head from side to side, flicking her soft, velvety tongue over and over his sensitive prickhead. She squeezed his cock knob at the base, and moved it with the motions of her head. Brantly groaned under the slippery friction between her tongue and the skin of his cock knob. The girl then rapidly slid her pointed tongue underneath his prickhead and ran it all the way down its length to his cock base.

The man's cock pulsed with the wonderful sensation. The girl's soft, wet mouth roved up and down the underside of his prick before sliding over to the top. Her warm mouth traveled along the side of his cock, then back down underneath. Nibbling and sucking, she licked up to his cockhead, leaving a trail of glistening wetness behind. Soon, his whole cock gleamed in the light. Jennifer returned her attention to his prickhead, licking over it again and again. She paid attention to every square inch of reddened prickhead flesh, using her tongue on it with tender loving care. There was nothing like a cock in her mouth to make the girl feel good about herself.

Now she formed her sweet lips in a small 0,

then fastened them over the hole in his prick knob. She pushed her head forward, and her lips slowly opened wider as the fat prick entered her mouth. Her smooth lips tightly slipped over his glistening prick skin. She pushed her head down until a little more than half its length was lodged in her hungry mouth.

Jennifer bobbed her head up and down. She sucked his cock into her mouth as she drove her lips down onto it. Releasing the suction while maintaining a tight grip with her slick lips, she pulled her head back up. The loose flesh was pulled up along with her lips. Then she drove her lips back down his steel-hard prick and held about six inches in her mouth while exerting a powerful sucking force. Sucking rhythmically, she twisted and turned the exposed portion of cock with her hand. Her hand pumped up and down his sensitive cockflesh, back and forth, slipping and sliding over and around its base.

Brantly groaned, "Yeah, baby. Ohhh, feels good."

Pleased with herself, Jennifer sucked and used her tongue on the underside of his cockhead. She frantically twisted and turned her head. She pulled and stroked his hard prick flesh with her lips, and her velvety tongue flicked rapidly underneath and around his cock knob. With her left hand, she fondled the man's heavy balls.

Swiftly, she took her lips from around his cock. Laying her tongue under his prickhead, she slid it all the way down to his balls. She began licking over his hairy ball-sac. She licked his balls, first one and then the other. Then she moved to the inner part of the man's thighs. The man moaned in delight as the hypersensitive area was licked and kissed.

Jennifer moved back to his balls and licked over them, thoroughly soaking them with her lips and tongue. She licked until all the hairs lay down flat on his loose ball-skin, then opened her mouth as wide as she could. She gently sucked his balls into her mouth, drawing his balls into it with a slow, careful sucking. First one ball and then the other plopped into her mouth. She hefted them with her tongue, rubbing all over and around them. The man's balls tightened up in pleasure. Her hand kept stroking the man's cock.

After nursing on Brantly's balls, Jennifer eased them out of her mouth. Her soft tongue slid back up the underside of the straining cock until she got to his swollen cockhead. Brantly put his hands on the back of her head, urging her on. He lovingly coaxed her into doing her best, to suck his prick as best she knew how.

"Suck it, baby, that's it. Suck it! Suck it good!

Suck my prick 'til I cum in your mouth. Mmmmmmm, that feels good."

Spurred on by his words, Jennifer began sucking him off for all she was worth. Her young face bobbed up and down his hard prick as fast as she could move it Her hair flew back and forth as her head sped up and down. Her hand jacked off what small portion of cock she couldn't get in her mouth. Her lips and tongue tried to satisfy the rest of it.

She pulled down the loose flesh at the root, stretching his cock taut. Her lips slipped and slid up and down his steelish cylinder of prick flesh. Her warm Lips sucked with incredible gusto. The man's prick twitched as he clenched his muscles in response to her handling of the affair. His prick seemed to expand at regular intervals in her mouth. The girl kept up her sweet sucking. Gripping the tense flesh as hard as she could with her lips, she pumped them as hard and as fast as she could.

Now she stroked his prick with her hand, jacking his cock into her mouth. She bobbed her head up and down, tightly gripping his pulsing cock with her locked lips. She held her tongue pressed to the underside. She was tremendously enjoying herself as her mouth was repeatedly filled and refilled with hot, horny cock.

Jennifer breathed harder and harder with the

effort of her sucking. She smelled the aroma of prick, and breathed deeply to fully savor its powerful heady aroma. She was becoming intoxicated with its aroma as she kept up her relentless sucking. Fondling and massaging his balls with her left hand, she stroked and kneaded the loose flesh at the base of Brantly's cock with the other. She sucked in building passion. Her cunt oozed cream as she gave the teacher a blowjob.

She closed her eyes for short periods of time as she satisfied her oral cravings with the teacher's cock. She loved its smooth, fleshy taste, and she was eager to swallow his cum.

Jennifer sucked and stroked his prick with her slippery lips in renewed vigor. Stroking the loose flesh with her hand, she pistoned her lips over his hard cock faster and faster. Every now and then, she pulled her lips up and locked them behind his swollen prick knob. There, she rotated her head. Flicking her tongue rapidly over his prick tip, she twisted and pulled her head like a calf sucking one of its mother's tit. She desperately wanted his prick milk, and she kept pulling his cock with her mouth in an effort to taste the man's jizz.

She had not much longer to wait. Her sweet mouth was taking its toll on Brantly's aching prick. He leaned back, thrusting his long cock as deeply as possible into the girl's mouth so she could suck and lick as much as she could take. He tensed his muscles, twitching his cock in pleasure. His rubbery prickhead expanded and contracted as the blood was forced into it. He could feel his load straining to escape the confines of his tight balls. His cock itched to release its load of cum. The sensations built up in intensity until he could no longer hold himself back.

"Suck it, bitch! Oh, you sweet, sucking bitch, suck me off! Suck my cum! Oh, I'm gonna cum in your mouth! Don't stop! Aaarrrrgghhhh, oh, oh, unnnnngh!"

Jennifer felt the man's hands grabbing harder on her head. She loved it as more of his stiff prick slid into her mouth. She moved her head slightly so as not to choke on it before sliding her face down again. She picked up speed, greedily gobbling and sucking on his pulsing, mouth-fucking prick.

She felt it twitching and pulsing as it prepared to shoot its load. The feeling so turned her on that she almost came without touching her cunt. The muscular spasms came in rapid succession and the wet, warm cum overflowed onto her waiting tongue. She sucked and licked with renewed energy as the cum spurted into her eager mouth. Wad after thick wad of cum shot into her sucking mouth, and she gratefully slurped up every drop of the delicious jizz. She had sucked him for all she was worth and now was collecting her due-a load of hot, steaming cum.

Spurt after hot spurt of cream squirted out of Brantly's throbbing prick and into her waiting mouth. Jet after powerful jet of cum streamed from the man's balls. Jennifer hungrily lapped it up, holding his jizz all in her mouth to savor its exotic, creamy taste. Her sweet, wet lips pumped his spurting prick as she milked him dry with her mouth. Oh, how she loved sucking cum.

Jennifer felt the man's body begin to relax. She slowed her sucking until finally, her head came to a standstill. Her tongue, however, was still busy swirling and licking his drained cock, which gave an occasional twitch in response.

After happily nursing on the teacher's cock, she slowly pulled the still-stiff prick out of her mouth. As her mouth pulled up for the last time, she sucked strongly to extract every last drop of his white cum. At his prickhead, she lingered a while with her pointed tongue swirling to probe his piss hole for any last traces of cream. Then she lightly slid her tongue along the underside of his cock. She licked all the way to his balls, then back to his reddened prickhead. The man lurched.

"Okay, baby, that's enough. Ohhhh," he groaned.

The girl looked up at him, smiling. They looked

into each other's eyes, contented smiles showing on each face. Jennifer held his cum in her mouth. She rolled the jizz around with her tongue, loving its exquisite flavor. She rolled it all over her tongue, pushing the cum around until every fraction of her mouth had been coated with it.

She swished it back and forth, then collected it all on her tongue. Looking straight into Brantly's satisfied eyes, she opened her lips and rolled her tongue out. The thick white load of cum quivered on her tongue. She was careful not to spill a drop, and carefully brought her tongue and the load back into her cum-hungry mouth before an accident happened. Closing her eyes, she swallowed.

Jennifer stood and straightened her dress. The teacher pulled up his pants, standing on shaky legs as he put his drooping prick back into his pants. His mind was blown, as well as his cock.

"Goddamn, Jennifer. That was good, baby." He kissed her on the lips, giving thanks.

"I'm glad you liked it, Mr. Brantly. I did." She blinked her eyes at him. "We'll do it again sometime, if you'd like to," she offered. "Your cum tastes good."

"You can suck me anytime you want to, honey.

With a parting smile, Jennifer went out the door. Mr. Brantly watched her fine ass shaking from side to side as she left. For a long while, he stood there with a dazed, contented look on his face.

CHAPTER 9

Jennifer slept soundly that night, satiated. When she awoke, she felt alive and refreshed.

As she left for school, she thought with a sense of loss that today was the last day of school. The summer vacation loomed interminably long before her.

Jennifer wondered who she would find to take care of her newly awakened desires all summer. One thing was for sure, and that was that she would be one grateful girl when school started back up in September. Then they'd have nine months to enjoy themselves before she graduated. She was amazed at the change that had taken place within her. Before this, she'd have never thought she'd be so eager for school to start back up.

Upon arriving at school, the first person she saw was her ex-boyfriend, Jake. She was filled with revulsion as she looked at the wimp.

"Hey, Jennifer! Where've you been the last couple of days?" he demanded. "I've been looking for you."

"Oh, h-hello, Jake. I've-I've been busy." She looked around, stamping her foot. The boy held no more interest for her after having seen how real men behaved.

"Say, how'd you like to go bowling Friday night? It'll be fun." He leered as he bent his face closer. "Afterwards, we'll have a little excitement."

As gently as she could, Jennifer told him, "Jake, I'm sorry, but I don't think so." How could she explain to him that now they were worlds apart? They could never get back together again. "I-I don't think we should see each other again. G-goodbye, Jake." She quickly made her exit.

Jake's face fell as he watched his prize escaping. He ran a little ways after her, calling her name. When the girl kept going, he slowed and stopped. Rick the whore, he thought.

Jennifer was walking past the office when Mrs. Johanson stepped out and touched her arm. "Hi, Jennifer. Let's go into my office." Her meaning was clear.

Jennifer's cunt tingled with desire, but she had a final to take. "I--I can't, Mrs. Johanson. I've got to take a final this morning."

The woman steered her into the office, saying, "Now don't you worry about that, honey. We'll take care of it for you."

Jennifer looked at the woman, wide-eyed and trembling. Her cunt took command of her brain. She floated into the woman's office.

Mary shut the office door and she went around her desk. She stood up with a package, which she handed to Jennifer. "Here. Go into the bathroom there and put these on. Be quick, now. I'm waiting." She nudged the unprotesting girl toward her office bathroom. "Oh, and put your hair in a ponytail while you're in there.

With her cunt oozing, Jennifer took the package into the bathroom. Her breath caught in her throat as she opened it. Inside were a black leather slave collar, a red quarter-bra trimmed in black lace, a matching garter belt, a matching g-string, flesh-tone nylon stockings, and a pair of red, open-toed high heels. Quivering more excitedly, the girl put them on, then tied her hair in a ponytail. She was hot and ready for action as she opened the door and re-entered the office. After taking a few steps, she stopped, startled.

Sitting on the couch against one wall of the spacious office were Mr. Hawthorne, Mrs. Johanson, Coach O'Reilly, and Mrs. Debra Cox. The latter woman was a young teacher Jennifer had seen around school, but had never met. She was blonde, petite and good looking. Jennifer quickly recovered and tried to stay cool as she walked to the center of the room. Her heart was beating furiously as she stood 'in front of them for inspection.

Appreciative sighs arose as the spectators took in the young girl's fine, slender form. Her tits were pushed up and out by the quarter-bra.

Her nipples were fully exposed. Her tender pink tit-tips were large and circular as they stood out in excitement. The tiny g-string barely covered her downy cunt bush. It stopped just beneath her clit. She looked very young with her hair pulled back. Noticing their admiring stares, Jennifer was filled with a wonderful sense of self-confidence. She found that she loved being the center of attention as their eyes studied her from top to bottom.

Mrs. Johanson said, "Jennifer, this is Debra Cox. She noticed you around the school, and liked what she saw. I thought you'd like to meet her." She paused. "Larry told us everything you did yesterday." Jennifer blushed. "You seem to have enjoyed yourself very much."

Hawthorne spoke up, "Yeah, she sure did. She liked getting fucked in the ass best of all, didn't you, Jennifer?" Jennifer shyly smiled and nodded. She was unable to speak. The man continued.

"Turn around and show us your ass, Jennifer."

She did as she was told. All eyes present stared at her firm, rounded asscheeks. The black g-string ran between them in her asscrack.

"Spread your asscheeks," Hawthorne commanded.

Jennifer ran her hands over her asscheeks, sending shivers up and down her spine. Then she spread them apart and bent over slightly to push her ass out at them. All eyes stared between her asscheeks. The brown, puckered ridge of her asshole was pulled on either side of the string. The soft pink flesh inside her asshole tantalized the viewers as it barely peeked out from behind the string.

"Pull the string aside. We want to see your asshole," said Larry.

Again, Jennifer did as ordered. Awed sighs were heard as everyone stared at the shit hole between her asscheeks. Her brown asshole twitched. It looked so soft, so tender, so tight. Every man present wanted to fuck her ass. Every woman wanted to lick and finger it.

Jennifer waited with the cool air caressing her asshole. Mrs. Johanson got up and went to her desk. She took out two eight-inch dildoes. They were of pink rubber, and very thick. She handed them to the girl, saying, "Here's what we want you to do Jennifer. We want to watch you play with yourself. First, pose for us like you are. Then, strip off the g-string and play with your pussy and ass. After a while, fuck yourself with these dildoes in your cunt and asshole. Fuck yourself until you cum. Here." She handed them to the girl. "Make it good, now."

Jennifer set the dildoes on the floor and she started posing for her audience. She thrust out her tits and cupped them. She ground her hips from side to side as she pinched her nipples. She seductively licked her lips and flicked her tongue in and out. Turning around, she caressed her asscheeks. Gyrating her ass, she spread her legs. She bent over and looked at the other people from between her legs, shaking from side to side. She turned back around and rubbed her pussy, thrusting it into her hand as she fingered herself. She then licked her lips, rubbed one tit, and fingered her cunt at the same time. Her body was taken over by thoughts of lust as she got hotter and hotter with each passing second.

Bending over to hide her cunt, she ripped off the g-string. As the audience strained to get a view, she turned from side to side, not showing them her pussy. Finally, she stood up and thrust out her cunt. Spreading her legs, she opened the tender pink fuckhole. It glistened with wetness. White, frothy cunt cream glistened inside on the swollen walls of her pussy. Before the people could look too long, she twisted away from them and began gyrating back and forth. She bent over and spread her asscheeks wide apart to let them see her asshole. Her quivering shit hole puckered and loosened in the girl's excitement. Able to take it no more, Jennifer threw herself on the floor and spread her legs wide.

Lifting her knees, she started rubbing her clit. Several long strokes later, she started running her hands over her cuntlips. Then she grabbed them and pulled them open to let the men and women see inside her pussy. She ran two fingers around her fuckhole, smearing her slippery cunt juices all around. As the fingers pushed into her fuckhole, she frigged her clit with the other hand. It was so good, she couldn't hold in her squeals of delight.

"Ohhh, yeah, oh, ahhhh, mmmmmm, oh, ohhhh!"

She moaned feeling her fingers opening her cunt and shoving inside. Her clit throbbed under her fingers as they flicked and rubbed it. Her fingers worked on her cunt, sliding all around. They slipped up and down her moist pussy slit, then back into her fuckhole, She worked her cunt in circles and from side to side. She thrust the fingers in and out faster and faster, while rubbing her clit. She was working herself into a frenzy of lust as her clit swelled and throbbed more and more.

Jennifer raised her knees almost to her tits, lifting her ass off the floor. Momentarily, her hands left her cunt and slid over her smooth asscheeks. She massaged them, then pulled them wide apart. She ran her fingers over her asshole. She circled it, then flicked her fingers back and forth, moaning in pleasure. Her other hand quickly slid over her tits, and then down to her clit once again. When she couldn't take the teasing anymore, she reached for the dildoes.

She quickly dipped one of them into her mouth. After licking and sucking the dildo to wet it thoroughly, she put it between her legs. She rubbed it up and down her cuntslit, pushing increasingly harder against her cunt. Spreading her legs farther apart, she centered the dildo against her wet hole. Her pussylips spread apart, and the dildo sunk between them. She was trembling in desire as she started pushing it into her cunt.

The big tip of the dildo opened up her fuckhole. She moaned as her cuntlips split widely to take it. She slowly worked it back and forth until the first couple of inches were comfortably inside her. Her cunt was as wide open as it had ever been before. She paused a moment before she started working with the dildo again. Resting with her eyes closed and a dreamy smile on her lips, she savored the throbbing pleasure coming from her cunt. Then grasping the dildo firmly, she pulled it back an inch. She pushed, first gently, and then harder as she forced it into her pussy. The slippery sheath of her cunt gripped the dildo tightly as her fuckhole expanded to take it. She couldn't help groaning aloud as it slid half way in.

"Oooooohhhhh, ooooohhhhhh! It's good, so good," she moaned.

Mary urged her on. "That's it, Jennifer. Oh, yes! Put it in. Oh, I can't stand it!" She lifted her dress and shot her hand into her panties.

Meanwhile, huge bulges had grown in Dave's and Larry's pants. Their eyes were about to pop out of their sockets as they watched the young girl forcing her cunt open with the dildo. First Larry took his cock out and began jacking off. Dave was not long in following suit. The other woman, Debra, sat there crossing and uncrossing her legs as she watched in utter fascination.

Jennifer pulled the dildo back, then shoved it deeper. Pulling back almost all the way, she was determined to take it all this time. With one long, firm stroke, she forced the dildo all the way into her cunt. She grunted as her hand touched her widely split cuntlips. Her cunt was stretched wide open and stuffed to the limit. It throbbed powerfully, sending pleasure waves rippling through her body. After resting for just a minute, she began a steady fucking of her pussy.

"Ohhh, goddamn it! It feels good! Ohhh, so good, ahhhh, mmmmm, fuck!" she panted.

The men and women stared hungrily at the young girl's pussy. Her cunt was stretched wide open around the dildo. Her clit stood up, throbbing and engorged with blood. Her fuckhole was stuffed so full that Jennifer's clit was pulled back and forth with each pump. They could see the bright pink flesh of her cunt. A thick, creamy froth coated the dildo and the inside of her cunt. They watched the girl fucking herself faster and harder, thrusting her pussy up to meet the dildos every thrust. Each time the dildo fucked deep, the girl cried out in joy. Now even Debra had thrown up her dress and was rubbing her own cunt as she watched.

Jennifer was experiencing extreme pleasure as she fucked herself silly with the dildo. She fucked herself hard, hammering away and grinding the dildo deeply into her fuckhole with each stroke. It wasn't long before her body started shaking as the pleasure multiplied under the steady cunt and clit massage. Shivers began at the tips of her toes and gradually traveled the length of her body as she came.

Her head jerked from side to side. She kicked with her legs, bucking her gaping cunt against the down-stroking dildo. Her muscles spasmed repeatedly. The juices came in a gush, trickling out of her fuckhole each time the dildo was pulled back. She fucked herself hard and deep until her climax lessened and the spasms came further apart. She slumped back with a contented sigh, leaving the dildo buried in her cunt. As her head stopped spinning, she looked with glazed eyes at Mrs. Johanson.

The woman said, "That was a good show, Jennifer, a fine show. My pussy's so wet, I want you to clean it, but not right now. Now we wanna see you dildo-fuck yourself in the ass." She studied the girl for a moment. "Hmmmm. Maybe you'd like someone to help you. Yes, I think you'd like that." She turned. "Debra, would you like to fuck Jennifer in the ass?"

The young blonde woman was filled with lust as she answered. "Yeah, I'd love to." Her face was flushed excitement as she unbuttoned her dress. It fell to the floor, and she stood there in nothing but high heels, panties, and garter belt and stockings. Quickly, she stepped out of her panties.

Jennifer peered through a fog of lust as Debra crawled over to her. Panting in heat, she observed that the young teacher was beautiful. She had long blonde hair and fine green eyes. Her face was small and cat-like, and a smile was on her perfect lips. As the lady squatted back on her knees, Jennifer saw her full tits. They were very lightly tanned, capped by big pink nipples. Her tits were big and firm, with a deep crevice in between them. Jennifer wanted to suck them, but now was not the time. The lady's whole body was lightly tanned to match her tits, and Jennifer could see a wisp of blonde hair between her legs.

Mrs. Cox said sweetly, "Now, you just lie back and enjoy it, honey. I'm gonna take care of you." She bent her face to the girl's cunt and inhaled the musky aroma of lust Sighing in happiness, she said, "I've been waiting a long time for this." Then she started licking around the dildo and over Jennifer's cuntlips, tickling the girl's asshole with her fingers. "Damn, you taste good." She quickly bent her face down, planting it between Jennifer's thighs.

Jennifer's eyes rolled up as Debra's soft, warm tongue went to work on her cunt. After cleaning up Jennifer's cunt juices with her tongue, the teacher licked between the girl's asscheeks. She licked up and down the soft crack before her tongue lit on the puckered brown shit hole. Her tongue lightly circled the rim, then began swiping back and forth over it. With her hands, she spread the girl's shit hole open. Her tongue began pushing inside.

Debra looked up, her lips and chin glistening. "Mary, bring me the K-Y, will you?" Mrs. Johanson hastened to her desk and she pulled out the ever-handy tube of jelly. She went back and sat down with her hands on the two cocks, which she resumed massaging. The men picked up where they had left off, fingering her cunt and fondling her tits.

Debra smeared the lube all around and inside Jennifer's asshole. Picking up the second dildo, she greased it, too. When it was coated with grease, she pushed it between the girl's asscheeks. After tickling the girl's asshole with it, she centered the dildo on target and began slipping it in. Jennifer moaned and started massaging her tits as her asshole opened and expanded over the head of the big dildo.

Jennifer reined as her asshole opened up under the pressure. It stretched wider and wider, until the tip of the dildo slid in. The dildo slowly moved in and out, pushing deeper with each stroke. The pleasure mounted with the wonderful stretching. Her breathing sped up as she excitedly moaned.

"Oh, yes! Put it in me! Stick it up my ass! Ahhh, oh, yes! Fuck me with it!"

Debra's breathing was also coming quicker. She stared closely as she forced the young girl's soft asshole to open up. The puckered brown ridge swelled and slid over the dildo. Working it gently in and out, she pushed a fourth of it into Jennifer's shit hole. She paused a moment to let Jennifer's asshole get used to it. Then she pushed firmly and relentlessly. The big dildo sunk all the way into the slippery fuckhole between the young girl's asscheeks in one long, steady stroke. The woman was gratified to see Jennifer's body jerk in response. "Oooohhhhhhh!" Jennifer moaned. There was nothing so good as feeling her asshole expanding and filling up with something hard and long. Her moans could not be stopped as the dildo was driven all the way up her ass.

Her legs kicked. She thrust her ass up to meet the dildo, loving it as her tender asshole was rapidly filled. When the woman began fucking her with it, she ground her ass from side to side in desire. Soon, she was pulling her ass down as the dildo pulled back, and bucking her widespread ass up to meet its every deep stroking thrust. She hunched her ass against it over and over again, squeezing and clenching her slippery asshole in ecstasy. When she felt the woman fucking her with the other dildo in her cunt at the same lime, she was overcome with joy. Bucking furiously against the two dildoes, she knew she was going to cum.

"Oh, I'm g-gonna cum! D-don't stop, oh, please

fuck me! Harder! Fuck me!"

Debra fucked Jennifer faster and harder until powerful tremors shook the girl's body. She quickly pulled the dildo out of Jennifer's cunt. Thrusting and driving the other dildo hard and deep into the girl's ass, she fastened her mouth to the girl's cunt. She feverishly slurped and licked the inside of the girl's creaming pussy as Jennifer's body was wracked by mighty convul-sions.

Jennifer bucked and groaned in her climax. She felt Debra's soft tongue licking her cunt as her cub throbbed. Her pussy spasmed, and she could feel the juices gushing out of it and into the other woman's mouth. Her asshole twitched, squeezing powerfully around the digging, driving dildo. Her body felt stroked from the inside out as wave after wave of pleasure swamped her senses. Moaning and nodding her head, she came hard. Her body was flushed with excitement as she rode her climax to its satisfying end. She sighed helplessly as she fell back and relaxed completely, the dildo still slipping in and out of her fully opened asshole. It was such a soothing feeling.

The woman kept hungrily sucking Jennifer's cunt, moving the dildo slower and slower. Finally, she stopped ass-fucking the girl with it. With a last happy lick, she sat back on her knees. Her cheeks and chin were smeared with pussyjuice.

Debra gently tugged on the dildo until it slipped out of Jennifer's asshole. The girl snapped her anus shut to expel it. As she lay back, feeling damn good, Jennifer happily looked up to see the other three coming toward her, horny and naked. As she watched, wanting more, she heard Hawthorne say, "Now it's our turn, baby."

CHAPTER 10

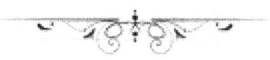

Hawthorne fell to his knees and pressed his mouth against Jennifer's. She opened her lips and sent her tongue to explore the man's mouth. Their lips wetly slid over each other. She was even more thrilled as the man broke off the kiss and straddled her face. Clenching her slightly sore asshole, she stared at the man's swollen cock.

Hawthorne's prick was reddened and throbbing as it neared her lips. A trickle of cum seeped from his cocktip. Jennifer opened her mouth and felt the hot hardness of his fucker pushing into her mouth. She swabbed the cum from his prickhead and began sucking. The tantalizing flavor of cum flashed over her tastebuds. Wanting more, she rolled her tongue around his cock knob and tried bobbing her head up and down. Since her head was pinned to the floor, she couldn't move it very much. Larry came to the rescue and started pumping into her mouth.

Larry moaned as the girl's velvety tongue went to work on his cock. "Mmmmmm, uuhhhhh. Use that tongue, baby." He was excited that he knew he wouldn't last long. He pushed part of his cock into Jennifer's mouth and then started moving it back and forth. A little more slid between her lips. He groaned as the girl gripped his cock with her lips and sucked gently on it. Her mouth was so soft and warm.

Jennifer was in heaven as the man fucked her in the mouth. She fondled his heavy balls as they swung back and forth. She jacked him off with the other hand while she sucked. With each out-stroke, her tongue swirled around his big prickhead. She opened her mouth fully each time his cock fucked in. The whole time; she kept her lips tightly closed as they slid down the length of the man's cock, and then back to the knob again. The next time she looked up, she saw Larry and Mrs. Cox frantically kissing over her head.

Debra was moaning in pleasure as Larry her cunt. Jennifer could easily see be the woman's legs to her swollen cunt watched in fascination as the man's fingers slipped and slid along the woman's She watched Larry's fingers massaged Debra's clit. Then they pressed hard her cuntlips and spread open in a V. The woman's cunt gaped open, and Jennifer could see the glistening pink pussy flesh inside. watched, the fingers pushed into the moist pussy. Jennifer felt a tongue going into her own cunt at the same time she cock swelling even harder inside e didn't know whose tongue was on her pussy, and didn't care. It felt good, and that was enough. She kept sucking Larry's cock, and soon she could feel his prick swelling up as big and as hard as it could get. With a rush of excitement, she got ready to catch his jism in her mouth.

As Larry's cock spasmed in her mouth, Jennifer glanced up to see him pulling the other woman tightly to him. Jennifer looked only for a moment, then quickly got back to the matter at hand. She felt spasms running from the root to the tip of his cock. She sucked hard, and her mouth was flooded with streaming cum.

She hungrily sucked and licked as his cock throbbed and spurted. The thick wet jizz flowed over her tongue and to the back of her mouth. It collected in a jelly-like pool as the cum kept shooting. The girl was in heat as she smelled and tasted cum. Her mouth wildly worked his cock over, her lips slipping and gripping to wring it dry. Her tongue swirled around and around his cockhead until she felt the man go limp over her face. She sucked softly until his cock was pulled out, leaving her with a mouthful of thick, warm wads of cum.

Jennifer hardly had time to savor the taste before the mouth servicing her pussy was removed. A stiff cock quickly replaced it.

Coach Dave O'Reilly slid his cock into the young girl's cunt as soon as Larry got out of the way. Her pussy was already slick and swollen, so he had no trouble in smoothly burying his cock inside her all the way to the balls. He moaned in joy as the hot, wet softness of the girl's cunt enveloped his cock. In response, Jennifer thrust her pussy up to meet him, groaning as her swollen cuntlips met the man's hard body. Both of them sighed in pleasure, grinding their bodies hard against each other.

Meanwhile, Debra Cox moved next to the girl's head. She took Jennifer's hand and placed it on her burning cunt. Jennifer knew what was expected of her. She started fingering the teacher's cunt. Debra moaned in ecstasy. She started feeling the girl's tits and nipples, pushing her cunt against Jennifer's hand.

"Oh, yes! Oh, Jennifer, rub my cunt! Yes, yes, yes, oh, yes!" Her body writhed in pleasure.

Jennifer lay happily with her legs pulled up as Dave fucked her. She ground her pussy at him, fucking him right back. She worked her muscles and held his cock in the slippery, clutching embrace of her tight cunt as his cock was pulled back for the next thrust. She loved feeling her pussy closing behind his swollen cock knob. Then once again, her cunt stretched wide open to take his cock all the way to the balls. Her nipples were puckered up in excite-ment as Debra's fingers played with them. The shivers of goodness that rushed through her body from her nipples heightened the pleasure considerably. Her hand worked over the lady's pussy. Jennifer wanted to give her the same pleasure that she had received.

Her fingers slipped over the woman's cuntslit. She tickled and cupped Debra's cuntlips. Slowly, she worked her middle finger between them and slid it up and down. She felt the woman's pussyhole, and worked a finger into it. After thrusting in and out several times, she withdrew her finger, only to replace it with two. As she finger-fucked the lady, she massaged her clit with her thumb. With this, Debra went wild. She ground her cunt into the girl's hand. She flexed her cunt muscles around the slipping, sliding fingers. Tossing her head, she moaned in ecstasy.

"Oh, yes! That's the way, baby, Fuck me! Ohhhhh, yeahhhh, oohhh, I'm g-gonna c-cum!" she squealed as her clit throbbed and exploded.

She pulled Jennifer's hand hard into her curd.

Spreading her smooth legs wider, she pushed hard against it. Working her cunt in quick circles, she spasmed again and again. Her nipples were standing straight out as her body convulsed, wracked by wave after numbing wave of goodness. Her breath caught in her throat as she bucked hard against Jennifer's wonderfully frigging hand. Too soon, it was all over. She flopped to the floor.

Jennifer wrapped her arms around the coach's face and she pulled his head down. Thrusting her cunt to meet every thrust of his cock, she opened her mouth and pressed it to his. Their tongues slid back and forth as their mouths met and locked together. Wrapping her legs around the man's waist, she pulled his body against hers. Together, they ground hard, enjoying the feel of every deep stroke. All the while her cunt muscles clutched greedily at the man s swollen cock. Her clit throbbed and the pleasure welled up inside her. As her cunt opened and closed under the ceaseless pounding, she came.

Her groans were muffled in the man's mouth. She gripped him tighter with her arms and legs. Her heels kicked, pulling him as deeply as possible into her cunt with each stroke. Her body tightened and convulsed. Her brain reeled with intense pleasure as her pussy spasmed and creamed. Her face flushed as her orgasm washed over her young body. Her hungry cunt pulled and sucked at the hammering cock inside it, and she mindlessly writhed and moaned in lust. Even in the midst of her climax, she felt the man stiffening on top of her.

O'Reilly was fucking the girl as hard and deep as he could when he felt his balls tightening up. The soft, moist inner walls of her cunt clutched wildly at his cock as the girl came. Her slippery cunt cream gushed out to lube his cock.

"Mmmpphhh! Mrnmph, mmmm, nnnph!" His groans were muffled and unclear, but their meaning was perfectly understood.

He slammed hard into the girl's yielding cunt. His cock spasmed. A strong pulse ran the length of his cock, and then it erupted in great, hot spurts of cum. He buried his cock to the hilt and ground from side to side. Then he pulled back, and he drove in to the balls once again. The convulsions ran through his cock and his body as the cum shot out of his prick knob and into the slippery fuckhole between the girl's legs. His brain fogged over with his lust. He slammed against her hard and dug his cock frank side to side again and again as his balls emptied into Jennifer's swollen pussy. It seemed like his insides were pouring into the girl through his cock as the powerful spasms wracked him through and through. Some gobs of cum dripped out of Jennifer's open cunt before the man fell against her, exhausted. After a moment of rest, he tolled off and lay on his back on the floor.

Mrs. Johanson quickly moved up and said,

"Eat me, Jennifer! Lick my ass!" She lost no time in squatting over the girl's mouth, facing her cunt.

Jennifer peered through the haze that clouded her vision and saw the woman's bulging asshole. Her light-brown anus was slightly agape. The ridge was wrinkled and looked sweet and tender. She smelled it. It smelled good. She licked it. It tasted good. She reached up, spreading the lady's asscheeks wide apart, and buried her mouth between them.

Mary's heady asshole aroma filled Jennifer's nostrils as she buried her face between the woman's firm asscheeks. The girl fitted her lips over the puckered rim of Mary's asshole. She ran her tongue around it, delighting in the warm, soft feel. After circling the woman's tight shit hole with her tongue, she licked over it again and again. Closing her eyes, she stiffened her tongue. Squeezing the woman's fleshy asscheeks, Jennifer pushed her tongue up the lady's ass.

Mrs. Johanson was going out of her mind with pleasure. "Ohhhh, Jennifer! Fuck, it feels so good! You know how-ohhhh, ahhhh-to use your t-tongue!

Oooohhh, honey, Uhhh, yeah!" she squealed. Then moaning more softly, she pressed her asshole onto the girl's mouth.

Jennifer pushed her tongue as far up the woman's ass as she could go. It was a strange but exciting sensation, feeling a puckered asshole opening up over her tongue and squeezing it tightly. She turned her head from side to side, working her tongue in circles. Moving her thumbs closer to the woman's little shit hole, she pushed and spread it open even more. Happily, she pushed her tongue deeper. She inhaled regularly and deeply, filling her lungs with the smell of the lady's ass. She was really getting into it when she felt Mary's hot breath on her cunt.

Mary pulled the girl's cunt open and saw the white cum spewing from inside it. She ran her finger along the girl's cuntslit and massaged around her clit. The girl twitched in pleasure. The woman shoved a finger into Jennifer's cunt. It slid in with slippery ease. When she took her finger out, she brought it to her mouth and licked it off. Satisfied that it was good, she pressed her mouth into the girl's dripping fuckhole and began wiping it clean with her tongue. Cum coated her tongue, and she eagerly slurped it up.

Jennifer moaned in joy, keeping her face buried between the woman's warm asscheeks. While her tongue licked and stabbed into Mary's asshole, hex hand almost unconsciously moved to the lady's pussy. She lightly ran her finger along the woman's puffed-up pussylips. She tickled the woman's cunt hairs. Then she traced the area around Mary's throbbing clit. Spiraling in, she started rubbing it. She could hear the woman's grunts of pleasure coming from between her legs. The lady began gyrating her cunt and ass against the girl's hand and mouth.

As Jennifer felt the woman's soft tongue swirling inside her cunt, she hiked her legs up over her head and spread them wider. Her cunt was fully opened, and her asshole was completely exposed. She felt the lady's tongue slipping out of her cunt to run up and down her cuntslit. It paused at her clit and flicked back and forth. Lips encircled her fucknub and exerted a firm sucking while the woman's tongue gave it an excellent lashing. Jennifer was almost ready to cum when the woman's tongue slid back into her fuckhole. Mindless with pleasure, she dreamily slurped at the woman's asshole. Her hand energetically massaged the lady's cunt.

After giving Mary's clit a thorough going over, Jennifer slid her finger along the woman's wet cuntslit to her asshole. Her finger slid back and forth several times between clit and shit hole before pushing into Mary's pussy. She jerked her finger in and out of the woman's soft, wet cunt. Swiftly, she pushed another one in to join the first. She finger-fucked the woman for long moments before returning to her clit. She pressed her palm against the lady's clit and began massaging it firmly. She kept her mouth working on Mary's asshole as the lady slightly raised her head and squealed in delight.

"Ohhhhh! Yeahhhh! Yes! Yes! Ohhhh, don't stop! Ohhhh, do me, honey! Fuck! Oh, yeah! Yes! I'm g-gonna cum, you bitch! Oh, eat my ass!" She buried her face back between the young girl's legs. Her mouth feverishly worked on the girl's cunt as she came with loud moans.

Jennifer felt the woman's body stiffen. Powerful tremors shook her through and through, and the convulsions hit her. Jennifer rubbed Mary's clit hard as she licked her ass. Mary's tight little asshole contracted and released again and again. Cream dripped from the lady's cunt and onto Jennifer's chin. The woman ground hard against the girl's face, twisting and jerking in climax. Jennifer was licking, sucking and rubbing for all she was worth when she felt her own climax welling up from deep within.

The woman's soft lips and tongue madly slurped at Jennifer's cunt. Jennifer felt Mary's lips circling her clit, while the woman's tongue wildly flicked over it. Jennifer's body trembled and shook. Her legs kicked and heaved. With long, low moans, she came.

"Aaaarrrhhh, uuuhhhh, oooohhhhh!"

Her moans were muffled in Mary's open ass. She tightened, thrusting her cunt into the lady's mouth. Her cunt spasmed repeatedly. Her pussy juices flowed out of it. She squeezed Mary's ass hard with one hand, while rubbing hard with her palm over the lady's clit. The two women ground their cunts into each other's face as they came.

Slowly, their madness left them and their reeling brains cleared. Both girls saw cunt cum flowing in streams right in front of their faces. Eagerly, they went back to work with their mouths. Jennifer licked from Mary's asshole to her cunt. Swabbing the entire area between the vice-principal's legs, she tried to get all the cunt cream cleaned up. Mary did the same. When they were through, happy smiles crossed their lips and cream glistened on their cheeks and chins. They looked about them and saw two stiff cocks and one more dripping cunt.

O'Reilly remembered his vow to fuck the young girl in the ass. He was ready to do it now.

"C'mere, baby. I'm gonna fuck you in the ass.

Jennifer thrilled to hear his words. Her asshole

was quivering as she crawled over to him and his fat cock.

CHAPTER 11

O'Reilly lay on his back, his cock stiff and throbbing. He thought of squeezing his cock into the young girl's asshole, and his cock pulsed even harder.

"Come on, honey. Get between my legs and spread your asscheeks for me. I wanna look at your ass first." He spread his legs, and the girl crawled between them.

Facing the man's feet, Jennifer was aflame with desire. The thought of once again having her little asshole stretched open and stuffed with cock sent chills running up and down her spine. Her asshole twitched in anticipation. She was at last going to get what she wanted most in the world--a good, hard ass-fucking. What she needed more than anything else was to be stretched wide and fucked deep by a stiff, throbbing cock. Bending forward, on her knees, Jennifer opened her asscheeks for the man.

Dave lay staring at the young girl's smooth, creamy asscheeks. Looking at the dark crack between them, his gaze centered on her asshole. Her anus was still greased and slightly swollen from the dildo-fucking that Debra had given it. The grease glistened in the light. Her little brown asshole was puckered up. He was going to love seeing his big cock forcing her little shit hole to expand over his prickhead and take his cock all the way to the root.

Fondling his cock, he said, "Jennifer, suck my cock a little first. Then I want you to grease my prick up and sit on it. When you do, face away from me. I wanna see your asshole opening up to take it."

Wanting his cock in her mouth, Jennifer was only too glad to oblige. She pivoted on her knees and fell on his prick. She licked the man's balls, then up and down the length of his cock. She paid careful attention to his swollen prick knob. She licked all around his cockhead and flicked her tongue over his pisshole several times. She ran her tongue up and down the underside until the man screamed his lust. Then she began sucking cock.

Jennifer pressed her lips against his prick tip and slowly slid down. She kept her lips tight, letting the thick hardness of the prick force them open. Soon she had gobbled most of his cock into her mouth. With her tongue swirling around and around, she bobbed her head slowly up and down. At the same time, she tickled the man's balls and pumped the loose flesh below her mouth. Feeling the heat of his cock filling her mouth was too much.

Spying the tube of jelly on the floor, she snatched it up. Hurriedly, she swiped the man's big cock with huge globs of the stuff. Smearing it all over, she squeezed and massaged his cock. Most of the grease was concentrated around his prickhead, but his whole cock gleamed with slickness. Spinning around, she spread her asscheeks and started squatting down over his rock-hard prick. Breathing hard, the coach held his cock by the base to keep it still and upright. He stared between the young girl's open asscheeks as her asshole touched his cockhead and began expanding over it.

Jennifer felt the thick warmth of his cockhead burning between her asscheeks. Relaxing fully, she squatted down. His reddened prick knob began penetrating her asshole. Her anus swelled to take his cockhead, sending shivers of pleasurable pain rushing through her body. Squatting further, she pushed her tender asshole down, forcing it to open up for the man's cock. She couldn't suppress her grunts of pleasure as her asshole stretched.

"Oooooooohh, oh, it's good! Ahhhhhhhhh, mmmmmmmm!

Dave watched in wide-eyed excitement as his cock knob slowly disappeared in the fuckhole between the girl's spread asscheeks. Jennifer squatted a little more, gripping her soft asscheeks and pulling them wider. Her asshole kept expanding until it gradually opened enough to fit over the man's big cockhead. Jennifer eased the pressure, grunting as his cock knob popped into her ass. Sitting still for a moment, she clenched her asshole, locking it tightly behind his cockhead. Then she began gyrating her ass in little circles, loving the feeling as her asshole slid around the man's cockhead.

Her little brown asshole expanded wider as it slid down the middle of his prick. Jennifer arched her back as she squatted, and his cock slid deeper up her asshole. Her anus opened even more as it neared his thick cock root. With a couple of inches left to go, Jennifer began pumping. She tightened her asshole as she raised up a few inches, pulling his slick cock flesh up. Just before his cockhead came out, she reined and lowered herself down. It felt so good as his cock fucked in, opening up the tight, slippery walls of her asshole as it did. She sank down a little farther than before, then raised herself back up again. Before the man's cock-could slip out of her asshole, she quickly reversed herself and slid back down, this time almost to the root. Her cunt was on fire as she clenched her asshole. She pumped back up, clutching the man's prick in the tight warmth of her ass. This time, determined to take it all, she pushed down hard. She squatted firmly, feeling his cock fucking deep. With a satisfied grunt, she forced her ass hard against the man's body. His big cock was inside her asshole all the way to the balls. Her slick brown asshole was stretched wide and deep. The girl ground down hard, loving it.

"Ahhhhh, it's good, ooohhhhh, yeahhh," she sighed.

"Oh, fucking right, so tight and warm, oh, Jennifer, baby," moaned the coach. It felt so good as the girl ground her ass against him with his cock buried to the hilt up her anus.

Jennifer stopped to rest for a moment, letting her asshole adjust to the size of the cock meat inside it. Throbbing pleasure filled her mind. Letting go of her asscheeks, she rested her hands on the man's legs. Then she pushed herself up, groaning at the friction of the cock sliding out of her asshole. Slowly, she squatted back down on it, filling her asshole to the brim with cock once again.

"Oh, that's the way to do it, Jennifer. Fuck me, baby, fuck me!"

The man held the girl by the waist. His arms moved up and down as Jennifer fucked her ass on his cock. He stared intently between the young girl's asscheeks as they rose and fell in a slow, rhythmic motion. He watched her asshole opening to take his cock all the way in each time she drove her ass down. He writhed in pleasure at the wonderful, warm tightness of the slippery asshole, and thought he was in heaven.

The girl dreamily closed her eyes, keeping her back arched as she sucked. A little smile was on her face as her ass moved up ax d down and from side to side. The more she was ass fucked, the better she felt. She was being sent into orbit with pleasure when she smelled the strong aroma of cock drifting into her nose. Opening her eyes, she saw Hawthorne's prick hovering a fraction of an inch in front of her mouth. Grabbing for it, she pulled his cock between her lips.

Her tongue swirled around his prickhead. Her lips wetly slid along its length. Her head bobbed up and down, sucking as much of it as she could into her soft mouth and slobbering all over it. Getting into it, she let go of his cock and held onto the man's asscheeks. She pulled him to her, madly working over his cock with her mouth. While she sucked, she didn't miss a single stroke with her ass. Debra Cox lay watching the lucky girl, envy apparent in her eyes. Her cunt was on fire with lust. She needed some loving attention, and fast. Whimpering, she crawled over to kiss the coach. They tongued each other for long moments before the woman broke it off. She quickly crawled around. Watching Jennifer's wet mouth pumping on Hawthorne's cock, she had to do something. Spying the man's swinging balls, she nuzzled up against them and started licking them. Stopping just for a moment, she got behind him and spread his asscheeks. Her mouth went straight for the man's hairy asshole.

Hawthorne's cock swelled even more as he felt Debra's warm tongue licking between his asscheeks. Pins and needles raced up and down his back. He looked down in time to see her wetting a finger in her mouth. Before he knew what was happening, she had pushed the finger up his ass. He gasped at the shock, but his cock swelled arid throbbed harder.

Jennifer licked and sucked while she ground her ass faster and faster against the coach. Her pretty ass pumped steadily up and down. She powerfully snapped her brown asshole shut around his cock root, jerking her ass and loving the Feel as his cock pulled back. But the best was yet to come. Before her asshole got to his prickhead, she relaxed and slammed her ass down hard. When Debra turned away from Larry's balls and attached her mouth to Jennifer's cunt, the girl went crazy.

Debra s tongue slid up and down Jennifer's smooth cuntslit, pausing at her clit, spiraling around the girl's fucknub and flicking over it. When Jennifer jerked her hips in response. Debra's tongue slid down between her pussylips and entered her open fuckhole. Her tongue swirled around for a while before sliding back up to the girl's clit. With O'Reilly's big cock fucking in and out of her asshole, another big cock sliding in and out of her mouth, and a soft tongue licking her pussy, Jennifer couldn't take it anymore. She came.

"Mmmmmpphhhh! Mmmmmmppphhhh! Ahhhhmmmmpppphh!" she groaned, her grunts muffled by Larry's cock. Wildly jerking her pretty ass up and down, she exploded like a keg of dynamite. Debra's head twisted crazily to and fro as she kept her mouth glued to Jennifer's bucking cunt.

Jennifer's asshole frenziedly convulsed. The breath shot out of her lungs. She gripped Hawthorne's ass, sucking harder on his cock. Her cunt spasmed, and her juices squirmed out of it. Her legs kicked, thrusting her up and down as hard and as fast as she could go. She pumped furiously, and her slippery, fluttering ass made Coach O'Reilly sigh in pleasure. The tongue in her cunt worked hard, and didn't stop until the girl's spasms had ceased.

Mrs. Johanson had been feeling somewhat left out, watching the action was no good, she wanted to be a part of it. Seeing Debra's silky smooth ass jutting out, she assaulted it with her mouth. Her tongue darted in, and she hungrily licked the woman's asshole. After wetting Debra's shit hole thoroughly, she licked the lady's cunt and slit. Debra's body gyrated in pleasure as she took her mouth off Jennifer's cunt, leaned back and went back to work on Hawthorne's balls. She stuck her finger back up the man's ass at the same time Mary Johanson's tongue went back into hers. Larry grunted at this new intrusion into his asshole. As before, his cock immediately swelled harder.

Though Jennifer was giving him an excellent blow job, Larry was becoming dissatisfied with her mouth. He wanted to fuck something. Pulling his cock out of Jennifer's mouth, he turned to Debra. After roughly pushing Mrs. Johanson out of the way, he got behind Debra and fingered her pussy. Debra put her head down as fingers worked in and out of her cunt. They were soon withdrawn, and then she felt Larry's cock pushing between her cuntlips. With a grunt, she took it all the way to the hilt.

Jennifer was momentarily disappointed at having Larry's delicious cock taken out of her mouth. She wanted to taste same more cum. However, the thick prick fucking her in the ass soon made her forget everything else. She joyously fucked back as hard as she could, loving it and begging for more.

Dave's eyes rolled back in his head as his cock swelled. His balls tightened. His body shook. He was covered with a thin sheen of sweat. Moaning, he pushed his cock all the way into the young girl's anus each time her asshole slid down to meet his balls. Her squeezing, slipping, sliding asshole at last took its toll on his cock. A long, low groan burst from his lungs. He pulled the girl hard against him, grinding up powerfully as his cock jerked and spasmed. Hot cum spurted deeply into the quivering fuckhole between the young girl's asscheeks.

"Ahhhh, annnnnggghhhh, uuuuuhhhhhh! Oh, oh, fuck, oh!"

Jennifer had known the man was going to cum in her ass when he pulled her hard against him. She felt his bestial fucking, and she ground her ass against him to meet every long, deep thrust. She clutched his cock as tight as she could in her asshole and lustfully fucked him right back. She felt his cock throbbing mightily inside her open ass as the man came. The powerful tremors transmitted themselves from his cock to her asshole.

She spread her cuntlips apart, frigging herself furiously. Her fingers pushed into her pussy and rubbed the slick inner walls. She held her cunt wide open, massaging her clit with her thumbs and the heels of her hands. As she felt the man going still beneath her ass, her body tensed up and convulsed.

Her body throbbed in orgasm. "Ohhhhhhh, oh, yes! Yes! Yes! Oh, it's-it's so g-good-ahhhhh! Mmmmmm... nnngghhh!"

Her asshole spasmed repeatedly around the man's cock, wringing the last few drops of cum out of it. She bucked wildly as she came, her breath coming in sharp gasps. Like a madwoman, she fucked herself in the ass with the man's prick and fingered her swollen pussy. Her mind was taken over by lust. She bucked and heaved, her whole body convulsing in extreme pleasure. Her asshole clenched and unclenched as she rode her climax to the end. By the time she collapsed, out of breath, every last drop of cum had been squeezed out of the coach's satisfied cock. She glanced at Larry and Debra just in time to see Larry pull his cock out of the woman s cunt.

Debra yelled, "Noooo! Don't stop! Don't take it out! Put it in me-please!" Her face flushed with excitement. She shook her ass wanting his cock back inside her cunt.

Larry chuckled, "Don't worry, bitch. I'm not done yet."

He looked at her hairless asshole, shining from the licking Mrs. Johanson had given it. His cock was coated with her frothy pussy juices, and he quickly pushed it against Debra's asshole.

"I'm gonna ass-fuck ya, baby!" he howled.

With one powerful thrust, he fucked his cock deeply up the woman's soft ass

"Ohhhhh! O-goddamn, it hurts! Please, oh!" she moaned.

Debra's upraised ass was helpless to resist the onslaught. Larry's big cock forced her asshole to open. Her asshole stretched painfully to take it. She was sobbing now as his merciless prick was fucked in again and again.

Her face was reddened and twisted in a grimace of pain as her asshole was ravaged. Her body rocked back and forth, shaken to the core by the impact of each hard, deep thrust.

Jennifer's cunt was still burning as she watched Hawthorne flicking his cock deeply into Debra's asshole and grinding from side to side. Feeling Dave's cock go limp inside her ass, she carefully raised up and let it slip out of her shit hole. She clenched her asshole, expelling his drained prick with a sticky, squishing noise. Wanting more of the action, she crawled over to Debra and Larry, leaving the coach lying mindlessly on the floor.

She went and knelt just behind and to the side of Debra's ass. She watched closely as the man's horny cock fucked deeply into the lady's asshole. Debra's brown anus hole contracted spasmodically each time Larry pulled his cock back for the next thrust. Then her ass was forced to expand widely to take his cock each time he fucked deep. The man held onto Debra's hips as he roughly fucked her in the ass.

Debra's moans had died down as the pain miraculously turned to pleasure. Knowing she was now subject to their wanton desires, she tried to relax. It wasn't long before her body was filled with a most wonderful fire. Her asshole opened and closed, again and again, as the man steadily fucked into her. Before she knew what was happening, her pussy was again creaming, and her clit was throbbing and tingling. The woman's moans turned to cries of pleasure, and she began fucking the man right back.

"Ohhhh. Oh it-it's g-good! Oh, yes! Ahhhh, mmmmmm, ohhhh, Larry! Fuck me!" She braced her knees and thrust her ass back to meet his every thrust. The slippery sheath of her anus clenched and squeezed the man's cock with every move of her fucking, bucking ass.

Jennifer, her heart racing with excitement, crawled underneath Debra. They lay facing each other, cunt to cunt. Debra lay on top of the girl, and they began grinding their pussies against each other. Their mouths opened and met. Their erect nipples slid over each other as they kissed and rubbed cunts. Debra kept her ass braced and spread, meeting Larry's every deep stroke with her soft, yielding asshole.

Mrs. Johanson, still unsatisfied, turned her attention to the coach. She kissed him long and deep. She fondled his cock and balls, trying to bring them back to life. Dave massaged her tits and fingered her cunt, but it was no use. His cock had been thoroughly milked by Jennifer's asshole. Mary gave up, and straddled his face, deciding she'd have to be satisfied with some tongue. Dave happily obliged, cupping her asscheeks in his hands as he licked and sucked the cream out of her cunt. Meanwhile, Jennifer, Debra and Larry were too occupied even to notice them.

While Larry fucked into Debra's asshole, the woman bucked just as hard against his cock. Her ass was humping and grinding as she savored the good feeling to the fullest degree. His cock slammed into her ass again and again, fucking her tender asshole hard and deep. Jennifer felt good as she humped her cunt against Debra's. But still, she needed a little more. She squeezed out from under Debra, and turning around, slid back in. She raised her knees and opened her legs wide to provide the lady's face a comfortable place to rest. She began licking and sucking the woman's cunt with gusto. Debra, feeling the girl's tongue in her pussy, needed no directions. She knew what to do, promptly burying her face between the young girl's smooth thighs.

Smelling and tasting the woman's cunt, Jennifer worked it over with her mouth. She spread Debra's swollen pussylips apart and pushed her tongue into the woman's shit hole. Her tongue was rewarded with a generous amount of cuntjuices. Her tongue swirled around and around, then slid up Debra's smooth cuntslit. After several long swipes, she licked to the lady's clit. There she encircled it with her lips and began sucking. While she sucked, she flicked Debra's fucknub repeatedly with her tongue. As she ate the woman's pussy, she stared at Larry's pistoning cock and Debra's swollen asshole. At the same time, Debra was sucking Jennifer's cunt.

Debra licked the girl's tasty pink cunt. She scooped up the thick cum inside Jennifer's fuckhole and smacked her lips. Her mouth ran up and down the girl's cuntslit before fastening to the girl's clit. She ground hard against Larry, squeezing his cock tightly inside her slippery asshole. She began quivering all over as Jennifer licked and sucked her cunt. Suddenly, she convulsed as her orgasm washed over her. Her moans were muffled in the young girl's cunt as she came, her asshole spasming and clutching at Larry's cock.

"Oh, yes, oh, yes! Fucking yes, mmmmmm, mmmmmmpphhhhhh!"

Jennifer's eager face was splattered with the woman's gushing cream. Joyfully, she licked and sucked feverishly. Her tongue traveled in long, swift strokes from one end of the lady's cunt to the other. With her head filled with the taste and aroma of creaming pussy, she felt her own orgasm starting from her clit and taking over her mind. She licked more furiously, and pleasure waves rolled over her body and swamped her brain.

As her body tensed and was wracked by convulsions, her cries, too, were muffled in cunt. Her body jerked and twitched. The goodness rippled back and forth from her toes to her head as the breath was squeezed out of her. Her legs kicked repeatedly, driving her gushing pussy hard into the woman's wet mouth. It felt so fucking good.

When it was over, she relaxed, but her mouth kept working. Debra was coming out of her climax, too, but she couldn't stop moving. Her ass was kept spread and busy, meeting every hard, deep stroke of Larry's fucking, driving cock.

Larry peered between the woman's warm asscheeks as he fucked her. He saw her asshole expanding and contracting as it met his thrusts. As the tight, wet warmth of her anus got to him, he mindlessly flicked her harder. Each time his cock fucked up her ass to the balls, he ground against her furiously, and the clutching heat made him sigh in pleasure. His balls tightened up, and his brain swam with lust.

Larry's mouth was not buried ma cunt, so his grunts were free to sound out. Howling in ecstasy, he felt himself starting to cum.

"Ahhhh, you hot assed bitch! I'm gonna c-cum in y-your ass! Ugggggghhhh, h-here it cums! Nnnnnngggggghhh!"

He pulled the woman hard against him, fucking deeply into her soft asshole. His cock leapt and spasmed, and gobs of warm cum spurted deep into the gripping fuckhole between her asscheeks. Her strong asshole pinched his cock in a vise-like grip, milking his prick from balls to cockhead. His cock flooded her asshole with cum, fucking in and out with a vengeance. Her powerful shit hole clutched and pulled the loose flesh of his cock until there was no more cum left in it. When his prick was dry, Larry fell against the woman with a groan.

Debra was pushed hard against Jennifer as the man fell down on her back. Jennifer didn't mind. She was content, the flames of her lust being temporarily quenched. She gently licked the other woman's cunt, loving the taste. It felt so peaceful to lay on the floor with another girl's cunt against her mouth. The grls gently tongued each other's pussy as Larry pulled his cock out of Debra's ass. The woman s asshole spasmed, and his prick flopped out. A squirt of cum was right behind it which landed on Jennifer's upturned face. She stared at Debra's swollen, cum-smeared asshole as she wiped the cum up with her finger and put it in her mouth.

They dressed on shaky legs, drained and satisfied. Jennifer left the garter belt, stockings and high heels on as she put on her dress, leaving off her panties. Her cunt and ass were fingered as she kissed each one of them before she had to go. She was saddened that she wouldn't see them for three more months.

On her way out the door, she was stopped by the voice of Mrs. Johanson.

"Oh, Jennifer. We'll be calling you this weekend."

Thrilled, Jennifer turned, whispering, "Thank you.

She had never been happier in her life.

Printed in Dunstable, United Kingdom